VILLAGE IN THE SUN

Herald Publishing House, Independence, Missouri

VILLAGE IN THE SUN

BY MADELYN GALBRAITH

Library of Congress Catalog Card No. 73-87640
ISBN 0-8309-0109-4

Printed in the United States of America

Chapter 1

It was a small village, half hidden by a maze of dusty grey-green cactus and stunted pepper trees. But after following a rocky road over the mountain, a visitor would find the first view of the pueblo as startling as coming suddenly upon a rose growing in a rubbish heap. Seen from above it looked like a giant piece of embroidery attached to the earth in an intricate pattern of vine stitchery with crewel work of trees and shrubs.

The plaza, centrally located, boasted a bandstand, concrete benches, flower beds, and grassy plots with winding walks between. Dominating this area was a fountain that sent its spray cascading into the basin below.

The church with its white-washed walls and tall spire contrasted pleasingly with the low roofs and brightly painted houses around it. These homes and their adjoining gardens crowded against each other, while those at either end of the road were forced to scramble up the mountain slopes where they clung precariously to their rocky perches.

The cobbled streets were too narrow to accommodate any vehicle larger than a cart, but the national highway passed directly in front of the hotel which was situated on an elevation slightly higher than the town.

At the other end was the schoolhouse. Its people proudly called this little village La Alhaja—the jewel. It was a quiet place except for the sounds of intermittent traffic, which were muted after the cars and trucks left the hotel and climbed the mountain behind it. There was little activity except on market day or when a bus brought a load of tourists bound for the ancient ruins beyond it. Then the village came alive and the streetlights burned late.

Opposite the schoolhouse lived Margarita Marquez and her son, Pasquelo. Mariano Marquez had for years been the mayor and only schoolteacher until, through his efforts, two rooms were added to the building and other teachers employed. At his death he had left his family well provided in that the home and plot of ground in the village and a small farm close by were free of debt, as were the chickens, turkeys, horse, and cow. With these resources his widow and child were able to make a comfortable living. Margarita was also the village dressmaker, thereby adding to their income.

The sun had not yet topped the peak opposite their front door when Margarita called Pasquelo to breakfast. He dropped his feet over the side of his bed and yawned. Half asleep, he shuffled through the kitchen to the well where he filled a clay bowl with water and washed his face.

"I have done the milking, but we'll have to hurry if we get the rest of the chores finished before the rain," Margarita told him when he returned.

"I'm not going to work at home today," he replied.

8

"No?" she asked, placing hot tortillas on his plate. "What are your plans?"

"The hotel needs wood, and I promised Señora Hernandez I'd get it this morning."

"Well, don't try to carry too much."

"I can lift more than Arcello...and he's two years older."

"Poor Arcello isn't a very good standard. I doubt that he has ever had enough to eat. Your papá and I always saw that you had plenty of nourishing food." Margarita finished her breakfast and poured water over the empty dishes. Pasquelo arose, took his machete from its rack behind the door, and started out.

As soon as he was gone Margarita cleared the table, washed the dishes, and went outside. She let the chickens and turkeys out of their coop, watered the animals and turned them loose to forage on the hillside, then began preparing the noon meal.

While the living quarters of the house were of adobe brick with tile floor and roof, there was a kitchen built apart with bamboo walls, thatch covering, and a hard packed dirt floor. One end of this narrow room was storage space for baskets of dried beans, corn, and other garden produce. The opposite end housed the outdoor kitchen. Bright blue enamel pots hung against the smoke blackened walls while herbs, garlic, onions, and peppers were suspended from a cord stretched across the room.

Margarita balanced a pot of water over a fire built between three stones. She measured beans into a clay bowl, washed them and poured them into the pot. A waist-high brazier stood near, but she bypassed it as it used more fuel than the small hearth. Assured that her dinner was well under way she took a hoe and went to the garden. "It will rain before night," she said aloud as she bent to her task.

Frank Faz had accepted the position of principal at a school without seeing it. Now he was on his way to learn what he had let himself in for. He wasn't sure why he had taken the post, sight unseen. Some friends who knew the area said it was a typical native village with its complement of progressive and backward people—but on the whole, not bad. He had been writing a column for an El Paso newspaper and found the distractions of the city hard to ignore. He had stuck it out for a year, teaching and working with youth groups, then decided that if he hoped to do anything with his writing he had better return to his native Mexico. First, he tried a school in Monterrey, later one in San Luis Potosi, and while both places were better than the one in Texas he was far from satisfied with either of them. It was then that he had heard of this small rural school and determined to try it.

These thoughts filled his mind as he guided his car over the rocks and brambles. Suddenly he realized that the road had narrowed down to scarcely more than a footpath. He was trying to back up the way he had come when he saw a youth bent under a load of wood, slowly moving down the trail. The load was strapped to his shoulders, steadied by a tumpline around his

10

forehead. Frank stopped and waited for him.

"Can you tell me how far I am from Alhaja?"

"Not far, sir, but you can't drive your car in through here."

"I can see that, but how do I get in? I'm the new teacher, and I want to see the school building."

"You'll have to go back. . . ."

"Come, get in and show me the way. Just put your load there on the floor." He got out and helped adjust it. "I'm Frank Faz," he introduced himself. "Will you be one of my pupils?"

"My name is Pasquelo Marquez, and yes, sir, I'll be in your school."

"Is it possible for me to see the inside of the building?"

"Oh, yes. My mother has the key."

A little later he directed, "Turn here. I live in the first house on the right, and the schoolhouse is across the road. Come on in while I get the key." Frank stopped in front of the Marquez home just as the afternoon shower began.

"Run to the porch," Pasquelo directed. Frank raced with him to the shelter, then paused to admire the flowers that stood in ranks on the tiered shelves. Bougainvillaea covered trellises at both ends of the porch and dripped in rivulets of pink, cerise, and copper.

"You have a regular greenhouse here," he told Pasquelo.

"My mother has good luck with flowers. Whatever she plants grows. Señora Hernandez says that if she stuck an adobe brick in the ground it would sprout into a house."

"That would be quite an accomplishment. She should use her skill to repair the one next door. It looks as though it could use a little magic."

"That place belongs to my uncle. He used to rent it until it began falling down. He and my aunt are quite old...too old to work on it, and he's too stingy to hire someone to do it for him."

"I wish it was in better condition. I'll need a place to live, and this would be convenient to the school. I see it has some fruit trees and plenty of space for a garden. I like that." Frank continued to study the house next door until the rain drove them inside.

The room into which Pasquelo ushered him was large and airy, although the windows had been closed against the rain. A tall wardrobe occupied one corner and an open cupboard displaying an array of colorful dishes stood beside it. One wall was completely covered with shelves crowded with books. A hammock was drawn up out of the way and a sewing machine stood in the center of the room, a length of bright cloth still under the needle.

"Sit down, Señor Faz. I'll call Mamá."

Frank carried a chair to the open door where he could sit and watch the rain. Pasquelo went to the back door and called his mother. She came in, wiping the water from her face and hair.

"Señor Faz, the new teacher, is here. He brought me home in his car," he told her.

"Oh? That's nice." Margarita discarded her apron,

12

shook the raindrops from her skirt, and followed Pasquelo into the front room.

Frank stared in astonishment when she came in. He had not expected to see such a trim, young-looking woman. Her wide, dark eyes reflected the sorrows of her people, but a ready smile formed dimples at the corners of her mouth. High cheek bones revealed her Indian ancestry, and black hair coiled on top of her head gave her a regal appearance. It took a moment for him to collect himself and divert his admiring gaze.

"Your flowers are lovely, Señora Marquez. I've been admiring them," he said after their introduction.

"I never have trouble getting things to grow for me. I think I've started half the flowers in the village, and I've supervised planting the school garden for the past two years."

"Perhaps you can tell me what condition the school building is in. Does it need any repair before classes begin?"

"I really don't know. Have you noticed, Pasquelo?"

"It's all right. Where's the key, Mamá? Señor Faz wants to see the inside."

"Don't go now, Pasquelo. Wait until we have lunch. It won't take long to get it on the table."

"The shower is over. Come on out back, Señor Faz. I'll show you my horse. Papá bought her for me when she was just a colt," Pasquelo invited.

Frank admired the animal and marveled at the elevated flower beds that poured streams of color over their rims. "Why are the beds on platforms?" he asked.

"Keeps them away from the chickens," Pasquelo

answered, "and the chickens' wings are clipped so they can't fly up to them. We grow some of our vegetables that way, too. The garden is over here."

Frank moved cautiously to avoid stepping on the plants. "You must have very fertile soil. Your garden is beautiful."

"Yes, we have good soil. Papá said our valley was the Eden of Mexico."

After lunch the vacant house and the school were inspected.

"This is a very small library," Frank said critically.

"I know. Papá had just begun working on it when he got sick."

"Were your books donated?"

"Some were. When Papá had the school he had us plant a garden and we bought books with the money we got for the vegetables we sold."

"Splendid! Perhaps we can extend that to raising a pig or two for market.... Now I want to see if your uncle will rent me his house. I'm sure I can repair it. I'd like to get it in shape while I'm here so I'll have a home when I return. Will you show me where your uncle lives?"

"Let me get my wood and I'll walk up with you."

"Leave it where it is and we'll drive."

"You can't. This is the stopping place. It isn't far, and we pass the hotel on the way to Uncle Salvador's."

Frank had a lonely breakfast the next morning at the hotel. The landlord spent the time leaning over the

14

counter staring moodily through the door. The waitress was courteous, but she served him silently. After observing them for a few moments Frank decided the two were husband and wife, and when he went to the register to pay his check his conclusions were confirmed.

"I am Henry Hernandez and this is my wife, Henrietta," he told Frank.

Henry was a portly man with broad shoulders and the arms of a blacksmith. His size was most pronounced in his girth. Although his body was inclined to heaviness its plumpness didn't extend to his face. His features lacked the grossness so often seen in large men and were as sharply defined as though chiseled by a sculptor. All this was crowned by a mop of unruly black hair.

Henrietta had evidently fared equally well on hotel food, for she, too, was generously proportioned. Her glossy braids framed a pair of sparkling black eyes, and her lips usually curved in a friendly smile.

"I'm sorry we weren't here last night to see that you were cared for. Were you comfortable?" Henry asked.

"Yes. I'd like to reserve the room for the next week or so. I'm going to be pretty busy for a while," Frank replied.

"We hear that you are going to repair Mr. Costello's house. You have quite a job on your hands," Henry cautioned.

"I realize that, but it's near the school, and I like having my own place."

"I envy you, Señor Faz, living next to Margarita

Marquez. She's a wonderful woman...my best friend," Henrietta added.

"She seems to be a charming person, but if I am to become her neighbor I'd better begin work on that house. Can you direct me to a hardware store?"

"What will you need, Professor? We don't have what you could call a hardware store. Most of Cosmo's stock is what he's picked up at old building sites."

"I'll need a hammer, a saw, and some nails."

"I have the hammer and saw. I keep a tool kit on hand because there's always something to be done around here. Let me call Pablo." He roared the name out the back door, and an old man hobbled in. Henry spoke to him rapidly in a dialect that Frank didn't understand, but the workman left and came back with a tool box. "Now here are the things to work with, but you'll have to buy the nails. I'm sure Cosmo has a few good ones. I'm sending Pablo along to help you. He's old and slow, but he's a good carpenter. If you have any trouble communicating with him call Margarita or Pasquelo. They'll interpret for you."

"Thank you very much, Henry. I'll see you at noon."

When he reached his future home Frank found Pasquelo picking up and stacking refuse. Pablo walked in and around the house, testing the strength of its foundation and supports. He explained to Pasquelo what was needed, and Frank went into the village to see how much he could buy locally.

The news of his presence, his future position in the pueblo, and his decision to restore Uncle Salvador's house had spread. When he returned he found that a

16

group of men and boys had gathered to watch proceedings. After a few minutes the younger ones joined in the toil.

At sundown Frank called a halt. "Doesn't it look good?" he exulted. "Come on, let's all go to the hotel for cokes."

Frank had to make several trips to Cuernavaca for supplies before the house was in order. When he returned later, prepared to stay, he found that Pasquelo had plowed his plot of ground and had it ready for seeding.

And his house shouted its welcome. Across the front porch clay pots held a blaze of color, and he rightly surmised that Margarita had shared her store of flowers. A formerly neglected morning-glory vine had been trained to shade the bedroom window. So vivid was the blue of its blossoms that it looked as though a piece of sky had found lodgment there.

After a brief survey of his home Frank returned to his car which Pasquelo was unloading with boyish enthusiasm. Margarita joined them and extended her welcome.

"Now this is a homecoming!" Frank said. "I know I'm going to like living here."

Chapter 2

Frank had his supper at the hotel and then stopped in at the Marquez home. After greeting Margarita he asked, "Where's Pasquelo?"

"He's helping Henrietta. Do you need him?"

"No, not really. Perhaps you're the one I should talk with anyway. I don't know if you realize it, but Pasquelo is exceptionally bright. I have been wondering what his chances for further education are."

"Well, of course, I think he's smart. Mariano taught him at home and had him reading and writing when he was four years old. He also tutored the boy after he started to school. He had great plans for Pasquelo... wanted him to go to the university of Mexico City. I wish I could carry out his dream, but I don't see how I can."

"It's a pity, for he definitely should continue his education. Perhaps I can coach him at night. I'll discuss it with him. But right now I'd better get some weeds out of my garden."

"Wait a minute... I almost forgot," Margarita said. "Roberto gave me your mail when I picked up mine."

Frank waited at the door until she returned with a letter. "From John," he said when he saw the handwriting. "He was my roommate and best friend when we were in college." He opened the envelope and read the letter. "Same old John," he commented when he had finished. Margarita looked puzzled, and he explained, "He wants me to translate some material from English into Spanish."

"Why doesn't he do it?"

"He doesn't understand English well enough, he says, although he speaks it fluently. Since my counselors knew that I intended to teach and hoped to work in the United States, they insisted that I learn the language well. John never had my opportunities. He cared for his parents until their death, then put a younger sister through college."

"Is this educational material he's sending you?"

"Well, in a way it is—religious education. There's another burden that he carries, although he doesn't consider it one. He assists his superior in conducting church services at a small mission. He was so excited about it when we were in college that it was all he could talk about. He wanted me to translate some pamphlets that outlined the beliefs of his church. It was a relief, in a way, for as long as I worked on this material he didn't preach to me!"

"It seems a lot to ask of you since you have your own work," Margarita said.

"Oh, I don't mind.... John is a very good friend. Now I must get home. I just remembered that I didn't wash my breakfast dishes. Do you know of any woman I might hire to keep my place in order and cook my meals?"

"I'm sure I can find someone for you. In the

meantime, why don't you take your meals with us? I would have suggested it sooner but I'm not a very good cook and I thought you might prefer your own or the hotel food."

"No, it all tastes alike, except some is a little spicier than others. And speaking of spice, who is that pretty little girl I see over here frequently?"

"That's Lola. Why do you ask?"

"She almost bowled me over on the plaza a few moments ago. She was running from a great hulk of a man. She gave him such a wallop in the stomach he doubled over. And she has a vocabulary that would put a truck driver to shame."

"Then Rosendo is out of jail," Margarita sighed.

"Who is he?"

"Rosendo is...is Lola's mother's permanent house guest, at least as permanent as the law permits him to be. He's been in jail in Cuernavaca, and I had hoped that he wouldn't return to the village."

"Evidently he hasn't found favor with Lola. From the names she called him I gather that in her estimation he's several grades lower than a worm."

"Did she get away from him?"

"Yes, by running to that young officer, Joe Morales. He wasn't in uniform but the man recognized authority when he saw it, for he turned and went back into the house."

"Well, I can expect Lola at any minute. She always comes here when there's trouble at home."

"Here she comes now. Say...why isn't she in school?"

"She's finished here and can't afford to go on to Cuernavaca."

"I see. Well, I must go home. I'm to have breakfast here tomorrow?"

"Yes. . . we'll look for you. Wait. . . it just occurred to me. . . . Lola could do your work as well as any woman. She's been taking care of her mother's family since she was a child."

"That's fine with me if you think she's capable."

"Before we decide definitely I'd like to discuss it with the jefe. It's likely her mother will want to collect her small wage unless we clear this with the law."

"Do whatever you think is best, Señora." He crossed over into his own yard as Lola bounded up on the Marquez porch. She tossed her black hair over her shoulder, but when she saw that it exposed a rip in her sleeve she drew it back to cover the tear.

"Come in, Lola," Margarita invited.

"What are you doing today, Señora Marquez?"

"I'm making a shirt for Pasquelo."

"It is very beautiful," Lola exclaimed as she examined the material.

"I hear you've been using something besides beautiful language, Lola! Professor Faz was amazed that you even knew such ugly words."

Lola's head dropped, and her bare toes traced the seams in the tile squares.

"What will Father Fidel say when you confess to this outburst?"

"It is not my fault that I said them, and I shall not

21

confess. Let that...that pig tell the priest. He made me say them!"

"I doubt that Father Fidel will accept your view of it. I really don't know what I'm going to do with you, Lola. I thought I had work for you where you could earn a little money for your clothes and perhaps for fiestas. But I don't think the professor will tolerate your swearing."

"Work for *him*?" Lola asked.

"Yes, he wants someone to come in during the day and keep his house, but I'm not sure...."

"Oh, Señora Marquez, please let me. I won't say those words again! I won't even talk if you don't want me to." Lola was sitting on her bare heels beside Margarita's chair.

"Well, I'll talk with Remundo and Joe about it. One of them can get your mother's consent. Now it's time for me to milk the cow and see that the chickens go into their coop." Margarita began folding the material she had been working on, and Lola darted about picking up pins and snips of thread that had fallen to the floor.

"Where is Pasquelo, Señora Marquez?"

"He's working at the hotel again. He's late, and unless he eats there he'll come home starved. I'd better heat the stew before I milk. And the chickens are scattered...."

I can't milk the cow," Lola said, flitting out the back door, "but I can do the chickens."

Pasquelo arrived while Margarita was lighting the fire in the hearth. She greeted him with "I suppose you're famished."

"No, Mamá, I can't eat another bite. I had supper at the hotel. What's the matter with the chickens?" he asked, hearing their squawks.

"Lola's trying to get them penned. Wait, Lola," she called, "you're scaring them. They'll go in if you just shoo them gently. Pasquelo, help her get them together again."

He obeyed, muttering "dumb girls." Quiet and order were soon restored, and Lola hurried off to find another task.

After supper she and Margarita walked up to the hotel to discuss the prospective job with Henry and Henrietta. Remundo Reyes, the police chief, came in while they were there and heartily approved. He agreed to call on Juanita and tell her about it. The mother was only too glad to be rid of the girl who disapproved of her domestic bliss.

"She's a lot of trouble—like her father. She fights with Rosendo until he's in a rage. I will come and collect her wages from the schoolteacher."

"Oh, no, you won't, Juanita! If I ever hear of you or Rosendo approaching Señor Faz on that account I'll put you both in jail," he warned her. Juanita was furious, but she had a certain respect for the law and knew that she dared not provoke the jefe.

"Now before we go next door to straighten the Professor's house you must have clean clothes," Margarita said the next morning.

23

"I know. Those barbarians down there did it! I'll go get my other dress."

"Well, while you're getting, don't get into another argument with Rosendo. And hurry back. . . . I want to start on Delfina's wedding gown today."

It was Saturday, and Pasquelo was lingering over a late breakfast, reading as he ate. Margarita had taken the white satin out of its wrapping and was spreading it on the bed when she heard agonizing screams coming from the direction of the plaza. She and Pasquelo started toward the sound but were stopped when Lola dashed up clasping her right arm close to her body. She slammed the door behind her and braced herself against it. "Don't let him get me!" she cried. "He tried to kill me, and he's broken my arm!"

"Rosendo, of course," Margarita took the slender arm and examined it gently. "It *is* broken," she said, "and I see that animal coming. Go into the kitchen and stay there. Pasquelo, run as fast as you can and get Remundo. . .or Joe or Henry. . .and hurry!"

At Rosendo's impatient hammering Margarita opened the door slightly.

"Are you trying to wreck my house?" she demanded.

"I want that girl!" he bellowed. "I've come for Lola!"

"You're not going to get her!"

"Lola, you better come here before I come in after you!"

"Stay where you are, Lola," Margarita directed. "And don't you dare enter my house, Rosendo!"

Pasquelo had slipped out the back door and raced up the hill. Knowing that Joe could usually be found at the hotel when he was in the village Pasquelo stopped there first. Joe was drinking coffee with Henry Hernandez when he rushed in.

"Joe, come quick! Rosendo is down at our house trying to get Lola."

Joe set his cup down and turned to face Pasquelo. "Trying to get Lola?"

"Please hurry, Joe! Rosendo's drunk, and he may hurt Mamá!"

"I knew it!" Joe said, clapping his cap on his head. "I knew there'd be trouble of some kind the minute Rosendo was turned loose!" He mounted his motorcycle and sped to the Marquez home. He entered the back door just as Rosendo thrust Margarita aside and barged in through the front.

"Did you want something in here, Rosendo?" Joe gave him a push that sent him staggering back onto the porch. "What's the trouble, Señora Marquez?"

"He was forcing his way into my house to take Lola. He has already broken her arm."

"Broken her arm! That little slip of a girl? . . . You've been back less than a week, Rosendo, and already you're in trouble. Those months in jail didn't teach you a thing, did they?" He yanked Rosendo to his feet. "Well, since you like to break things, I think I'll suggest that you be given the job of breaking rocks for the new road over the mountain. Perhaps a year at that will satisfy your craving."

Lola ventured out fearfully. "Is he gone?" she asked.

"Yes, and I doubt that he'll be back very soon. Here, let me help you wash up. We'll have to get you into Cuernavaca right away. If we only had a resident doctor, or even a nurse. You can't wear that dress; it's almost torn off you."

"I know. He did it when he struck me, and I don't have any other."

"Well, I'll run up to the village and see if Señora Valdez has anything that will do until I can make you one. And how am I going to get you into Cuernavaca? The bus isn't due for three hours and that arm should be set immediately." Margarita was talking to herself as she stepped off the porch.

"No problem, Señora Marquez. I'll take you." Frank had heard the news in the village and hurried home to offer his services.

"Thank you, but first I must buy Lola something to wear to Dr. Jaime's office," Margarita said. She hurried to the small dress shop and when she returned Frank had the car out. Lola changed into the new dress and was soon seated in the car, a pillow supporting her injured arm.

The doctor gave Lola an injection for pain and then applied splints. On the way home she slept in the rear seat while Margarita and Frank discussed her future.

"It won't be safe for her to go home. When Rosendo is turned loose he'll be back here to cause more trouble. In the meantime Juanita will have another man,"

Margarita predicted. "She's done it before."

"Where will Lola go, if not to her home?"

"She'll come to me, of course. I've been thinking for some time that I should adopt her. She really should be taken out of that environment."

"Wouldn't that put a tremendous burden on you?" Frank asked.

"No, I can manage. I'll be like the woman I read of once when we were living in Laredo. The family was very poor, but the mother would never turn anyone away from her table. When someone asked how she managed she said, 'I just take one piece of bread . . . and I add a little water to the soup.' That's what I'll do if it's ever necessary."

"That may not be wise," he cautioned.

"I love children," she said. "I was sorry that I didn't have more. Pasquelo has always been such a delight."

"Yes, but he's your own. You've had him all his life. Lola is a young woman."

"She's fourteen—old enough to be a companion to me," Margarita insisted.

"You're determined to see a bright side to the situation, aren't you?"

"That's better than looking for a storm in every fleecy cloud, Professor," she said, and smiled at him.

———

One afternoon several weeks later Lola sat on the side of the bed watching Margarita at the sewing machine. "What is that pig . . . Rosendo . . . doing now, I wonder."

"I surmise that if he isn't in jail he's working on the road as Joe predicted."

"Do you know what I'm going to do as soon as my arm mends? I'm going to hunt that beast and shoot his arm off!"

"Lola, what a terrible thing to say!" Margarita cried.

"And I may take a piece out of his liver, too. Juanita says it's his liver that makes him so mean, so I'll shoot a hole in it...just a little hole," she hastened to add at Margarita's look of amazement. "Just big enough to let the meanness out so he won't beat me when I go home."

"Lola, you must not even think of shooting anybody!"

"Why? He beat me and broke my arm."

"You just can't go around shooting people," Margarita reasoned. "But there's no need to discuss your going home, for you don't have to leave here. Judge Peña has arranged with your mother for you to live with me."

Lola was off her perch like a bird in flight. "You mean I don't have to go back...ever?" she exclaimed, bending over Margarita's chair. "I can live in this beautiful house always?"

"Always. And to insure your future you had better agree to my adopting you. Your mother has consented to that, too."

"Adopt? Then I'll belong to you, like Pasquelo?"

"Exactly."

"And you'll be my mother, too!" Her free arm was

around Margarita's neck, her face pressed close. "Oh, my little Mamã...you will see how I will work for you!"

"I'm not concerned about the work. What does worry me is that you have such wicked thoughts."

"How wicked?"

"Like shooting people. You should never even consider such things."

Lola thought for a moment before replying. In her old neighborhood the eye-for-an-eye code was often observed. "I won't shoot anybody if you don't want me to," she said at last.

"Good," Margarita said, smiling. "Now it's time for me to start supper. Do you think you can light the fire on the hearth? I want to heat the beans."

"Why not? I can do many things with one hand," Lola assured her. "And I'll hurry."

"There's no need to rush...and do be careful not to hurt your arm," Margarita cautioned.

So Lola became a member of the Marquez household. When consulted about it Pasquelo agreed. "She's okay...for a girl," he said.

The police chief came by occasionally to see if all was well, but his young deputy was a regular visitor. Margarita was not blind to this and watched anxiously as other young men of the village became aware of Lola's development.

"I dread the time when she begins to notice the boys," Margarita confided to Henrietta.

"After her earlier experience I doubt that she will be

29

eager for masculine company. If she ever does decide to marry I'm betting on Joe."

"He's been showing a lot of interest," Margarita admitted.

"I'll say he has!" Henrietta exclaimed.

Chapter 3

"What do you expect to do with your life, Pasquelo?" Frank asked one evening. The boy often came to talk with his neighbor or merely to sit in silent companionship.

"I'd like to go to college, but I know I can't. I'd like to teach school or work in a bank as Papá did."

"I'm glad you're ambitious. I discussed this with your mother some time ago, and she doubted that she could manage even a school in Cuernavaca. But I've been doing some thinking, and if I can swing this we'll be doing a lot of studying at night. Let's set our sights on college and work toward that."

"But how can it be possible?"

"Pasquelo, I have a friend who often helps boys get an education. I thought he might assist you."

"Is he a rich North American?"

"No, he's Mexican, and he isn't rich... well, by some standards I suppose he is. He has a chicken ranch north of Mexico City. He's always been a good friend to boys and young men who want more education than they can pay for."

"And you think he might help me?"

"He may help you help yourself. He doesn't dole out charity. He told me once that people seldom appreciate it—that they never place much value on something they've made no effort to get for themselves. The worth of a thing is usually gauged by the amount of effort expended on getting it."

"He sounds like a good man."

"He's one of the best. I think I'll visit him this weekend and see if he can provide some help for you."

Frank left his car in front of the house and walked down to the chicken runs where he felt sure he would find Grant Bera. "Still working the hens overtime, I see," was his greeting.

Grant turned to face him. "Why, Frank, what a surprise! I was thinking of you only this morning, wondering if you were happy in your new location."

"There have been problems, but they are beginning to clear up. I have a comfortable little house, pleasant neighbors, and interesting students."

"Good. Let me wash up; then we'll go inside and talk."

"No, I don't want to interrupt your work."

"My employees can carry on without my supervision. I was just doing a routine check."

"You've made some changes since I was here. I don't think you had your hens separated before."

"No, the cages are new. I went across the river with Ed Lozano. He's in this business in Monterrey. He had just started and wanted to get the latest on chicken raising from a man he knew in Texas. He persuaded me to go with him. This Mr. Moore has a huge operation in Houston. His chickens never touch the ground. From the time they're hatched until they're killed they live in floored cages."

"What's the advantage of that? It seems to me they would be better off outside eating seeds and berries."

"Seeds and berries aren't all they eat. By penning them I can give them the feed that will produce more flavorful meat and, of course, it's cleaner. With separately housed laying hens I can soon learn which ones are producing and which are merely taking up space."

"I can see the advantage, but isn't it costly?"

"It pays in the long run. Now let me show you my prize cows."

"You're in the cattle business, too!" Frank exclaimed.

"Not really. I like to have growing things about me, animals as well as people. And since I have to feed them, I may as well feed good stock."

The two men went from one part of the ranch to the other, and on the way back to the house Frank broached the subject that had prompted the visit.

"Grant, do you have a boy in school now?"

"Yes, I have two. One is in the university in the City, and the other is in secondary school at Monterrey. Why do you ask?"

"I have a youngster in one of my classes who needs some help."

Grant was thoughtful for a moment, then said, "It's lunchtime, and I'm hungry. We'll discuss your business later. Here comes Pepito to tell us that the meal is ready. Let's go in."

While they were at the table Grant drew Frank out about his village and its people. Then he said, "Now let me hear about this boy who wants to further his education."

"He's my neighbor. His mother is a widow. From our first meeting I've felt a sort of responsibility for Pasquelo—perhaps because, in a way, I supply the male companionship he had with his father. He's extremely bright, and if he has the proper education he should do well. His father was evidently an educated man. He held some sort of office in a bank in Laredo, Texas."

"I see. Will his mother be willing for him to come here to live?"

"I don't know. It would be a difficult decision for her to make, but if that's the condition she might consent."

"I've almost had to make that a condition, Frank. As you know, I've helped a good many boys get an education. Or perhaps I should say I've tried to help. With some, it didn't take. They had the ability but not the staying power necessary for further schooling. In other instances the parents weren't interested in the son's fitting himself for something besides selling lottery tickets and kept him at home at the least excuse. So now I have a rule; the boy must live here where I can see that he applies himself. I told you I had a student in Monterrey. I'm paying his expenses for the rest of the school year; then his family will take over."

"Well, I can see your point. You certainly don't want to throw money away. I'll talk this over with Señora Marquez. She's very ambitious for her son, so she may agree to the plan."

"I'd like to meet both of them."

"That's easy. Come visit me. . . . They live next door."

The next Friday Grant visited Frank and the Marquez family. When the plan for Pasquelo's leaving home was brought up, Margarita was stunned, but the boy was thrilled at the thought of living in Mexico City.

"He's never been away from me, Mr. Bera. . . . I just don't know. I'll have to think about it," Margarita said.

"I know you must, and there's no rush about making the decision. As soon as you do, however, let me know so I can make the necessary preparations."

Although months passed, when the time came for Pasquelo to leave, Margarita still was not emotionally ready for it. Grant drove down to get him.

"I see your bags are on the porch, Pasquelo. I'll put them in the car while you tell your mother good-bye."

Margarita walked with Pasquelo to the car and stood watching until it was out of sight, then turned to find Frank close behind her.

"Let's go up to the hotel and treat ourselves to one of Henrietta's indigestible concoctions," he suggested.

"Thanks, but Lola and I have our evening chores."

"Well, tell Lola not to cook for me tonight. I'll have supper with Henry and Henrietta."

He visited until Henry closed the hotel for the night, then walked down to the plaza and talked with the young men there until the group disbanded and went home. He sat watching several apparently abandoned children play around the fountain. At last they grew tired and made their way to the garage where they bedded down for the night in a deserted car. He looked at his watch—midnight! He knew he should be in bed, but he was too restless to settle down and decided to walk past the hotel to the highway over the mountain. He often took this walk in daytime and the view of the village basking in the sun always pleased him. Perhaps this same picture in the light of the full moon would have a calming effect.

As he neared the hotel he heard a rasping sound coming from the porch and stopped to investigate. He found a small boy crouched against a pillar of the verandah. When he picked the child up he discovered that he was burning with fever and breathing with great difficulty.

"What shall I do?" he asked aloud. "I certainly can't leave you here, but what will I do with you if I take you home?" He hurried on, his footsteps resounding on the cobblestones. When he got as far as the Marquez house he saw Margarita sitting on the porch steps.

"Senora...am I glad to see you! I wouldn't have

36

roused you, but since you're awake I want to enlist your help."

"What have you there, Professor?"

"A baby."

"A baby?"

"Well, maybe not a baby...but a very small child. He was crouched against a pillar of the hotel porch."

"Bring him in, but wait until I send Lola back to Pasquelo's room to finish the night."

Lola refused to go to bed and worked with Margarita, using the remedies she had tried on her own brothers and sisters, but to no avail. Margarita sent Frank for the herb woman, and the three of them worked over the child while Frank kept the kitchen fire going and set the coffee on to brew. Toward morning the fever lessened and the little patient's breathing became easier. At last he slept, and the four sat down with their steaming cups to discuss the event.

"Whose child is he?" Señora Garza, the herb woman, asked.

"I have no idea," Frank replied and told about finding him.

"I've never seen him before, have you?"

"Maybe he's one of those little beggars that hang around the plaza," Lola suggested.

"What kind of woman would leave a sick baby out at night?" Frank asked.

"The same kind that mothered those who run through the village hungry and half naked," Señora Garza replied.

"Do you know what we need for Alhaja? We need a

place where these children can be sheltered and cared for. Why hasn't this been done?"

"I don't suppose anyone ever thought of it, Señor Faz."

"Well, it's time someone did." Frank arose and went toward the bed where the child lay. "Now you ladies have been up most of the night. I'll take the boy home with me so you can get some rest."

Margarita sprang to her feet. "No, no, leave him where he is. You can't take him out in the cold air."

"Well," Frank hesitated, "if you say so. I'm sure you know best. But I didn't intend to put an additional burden on you."

"He's no burden! Yesterday I lost Pasquelo. Perhaps in his place, the good Lord sent me little . . . Gallo."

"Gallo?"

"Yes, he came to me before the rooster's crowing."

"And you want to care for him?"

"If God wills," she replied.

Chapter 4

"Señor Faz, you got only one letter, but it's a fat one. It's from Señor Acosta." Lola paused to read the return address before surrendering the envelope. She took a lively interest in all her employer's affairs.

Frank looked at it briefly and handed it back. "Put it on my desk, Lola. I haven't time to read it now. I want to transplant these roses before I stop."

An hour later he took John's letter to the porch where, hopefully, he could read it without interruptions from Lola. She had improved, but at times she still irritated him. She had few temper tantrums, but since the Marquez household ran so smoothly there was little occasion for angry outbursts.

"More translations," he mused, "and I'm not in the mood." He was agreeably surprised when no clippings fell out. After the usual preliminaries John plunged into the reason for his long letter.

I'm sure you remember attending a lecture on Mexican archaeology by a Dr. Harle while we were in college. He is now teaching in the university, and when I learned that he was giving a series of illustrated lectures I went to hear him. He is as eager as ever to discuss what he calls Mexico's "glorious past." Do you recall how he fired our enthusiasm and we declared that some day we would make a tour of the ruins? Well, what are we waiting for? I have seen Teotihuacan several times and I never tire of visiting the site, but think of the many others—El Tajin,

Zempoala, Chichen Itza, Palenque! As I remember Grant Bera and Les Cortez were as eager as we were. Les is in Alaska, but why can't you, Grant, and I take the trip? I'll call Grant and see how he feels about it. We can go in my car, and with three of us sharing the expense it shouldn't cost any of us too much.

According to Dr. Harle, Mexico is one vast archaeological treasure house and we'll have to be selective in choosing the areas to be covered, for I have some private tutoring to do in five weeks. If you and Grant agree on the tour I hope we can leave not later than next Sunday. Call me as soon as you decide.

"Now that isn't a bad idea," Frank told himself. "I'm sure that Margarita would see that Lola took proper care of the place. I'll go over and ask her now."

Margarita was sitting on the porch sewing when he joined her. He had hardly taken his seat on the top step when Gallo crawled onto his knee.

"If you keep growing, Gallo, you'll soon be able to take me on your knee. You've done wonders with him, Señora. He doesn't look like the child I brought to you a short time ago."

"I wish I knew his name. He can't go through life answering to that stupid label I put on him the night he came, even though it does fit. He gets me up every morning when the rooster crows."

"He should have another name, but I have an idea he'll always be called 'Gallo.' How in the world people can go off and leave a child like him....I'm still thinking of a home for such unwanted children. Which reminds me, as I sat on the hotel balcony talking with Henry last night I noticed a girl with the boys who hang around the plaza. She's larger than any of them and seems able to take care of herself. We watched her for quite a while. . . . She always beat the boys to any spot where the possibility of a handout seemed promising."

"A girl?" Margarita exclaimed.

"Yes. She wore a pair of patched levis and a man's pullover sweater. It came nearly to her ankles. The sleeves hung down almost as far and she had to keep pushing them up in order to use her hands. She had her hair—which is exceptionally long—tied back with a dirty ribbon. When I left the hotel she was asleep with the boys on the concrete porch."

"I wonder why they were sleeping at the hotel. Usually they stay in the abandoned cars at Bonificio's."

"I heard them talking about a late bus. I suppose they were waiting for it," Frank explained.

"I'll ask Henrietta about the girl. She knows most of those youngsters—in fact she feeds them half the time."

Frank arose and stretched his arms over his head. "I'm glad I'm through with school for a while. I need a break."

"Have you decided what you're going to do with your leisure time?" Margarita secured the last button on the shirt she was making.

"Yes, I have. That's why I came over. I had a letter from John. He proposes a tour of some of the ruins south of here."

"That doesn't sound like much of a vacation to me. Haven't you seen Teotihuacan?"

"No."

"It isn't far from Mexico City. Visit it and you can

41

skip the rest. When you've seen one, you've seen them all." Margarita dropped her sewing into the basket beside her.

"I'll have to disagree, Señora—they aren't all alike. When I was in college I saw some slides of temples and pyramids hidden for centuries but recently uncovered. Some of them were magnificent. The lecturer had half his listeners ready to grab a spade and start digging, and I was among them. Time has cooled my ardor, but John met the man again and is all fired up about reviving the tour we planned then. If I go do you think Lola can take care of my garden and flowers?"

"I can do it very well!" Lola answered from the doorway.

"Of course we'll look after your place, Frank. How soon will you leave?"

"By the end of the week. I think I'll go call John now."

Margarita and Lola were still on the porch when he returned. "We're leaving Friday," he told them. "I'm to meet John in Mexico City tomorrow, so I'll have to hurry and pack."

When Frank backed his car into the road the next morning his neighbors waved good-bye from their front yard.

"Don't forget to check on that girl at the plaza," he called through the car window. "I'll be staying at Grant's place for a night or two and, if possible, I'd like to hear what success you've had before I leave."

42

Chapter 5

John was waiting in front of the hotel when Frank drove up.

"I refuse to do any translating while we're on this trip," was his greeting as they embraced.

"Don't tell me you didn't enjoy doing those," John charged.

Frank rubbed his chin thoughtfully. "I won't go that far," he countered. "Let's say that I found them interesting. But there's one thing I want to challenge. You said those quotations were from the Bible. Now I checked, and most of them are not there. I asked Father Fidel if they were in his version and he said very definitely that they were not. And stupid as I am about things religious, I know that there's no reason to translate any part of the Bible into Spanish, for that was done centuries ago."

"Did I say the quotations were from the Bible?"

"You wrote, and I quote, 'Regardless of what your village priest says, those lines are scripture.'"

"They are scripture. Those passages I've been sending you are taken from the Book of Mormon," John explained.

"I've been translating the Book of Mormon?" Frank demanded.

"Excerpts from it, yes. And don't look at me as

though you had committed all seven deadly sins with one stroke of your pen or as though I'm an accomplice. But here, let's go inside and have lunch. I'm not licensed to preach on the street."

Frank followed him to a table where they gave their orders, then John returned to their discussion.

"You aren't the first man to recoil at the mention of the book, and those who react that way are invariably the ones who have never read it." John was silent while the waiter served them, then continued his explanation. "I tried to interest you in the book while we were in college, for to me it's a wonderful history."

"History?"

"Yes, the history of our ancestors. The author who wrote *Columbus Came Late* was right—he did come several centuries late, for civilizations had flourished and disappeared from the continent long before Columbus was born."

Frank finished his dessert and leaned back. "John, in trying to learn what I was translating...and I'll confess that many of the passages you sent me aroused my curiosity...I read the King James and the Catholic versions of the Bible. I found it interesting that some of the old fellows mentioned there are living again in people I know. Take Paul, for instance. In some ways you are very like him, and I believe the Roman ruler's charge against him can be directed toward you— much learning has made you mad. I am thinking now of your wild tale about an angel appearing to a man and telling him about a record engraved on gold plates."

"Perhaps I've told that story too often...or unwisely...but I do want my family and friends to share in the joy my faith has brought me. When you wouldn't listen to me, I hit on this plan of getting you to translate into our language some of our most convincing arguments. The entire book was put into Spanish years ago."

"Why, you fraud!" Frank laughed. "And you had me poring over that for hours!"

"It was a mean trick, wasn't it? But I felt sure you would profit from the experience."

"I'll have to admit I know more about the Bible...and your religion...than I would ever have learned otherwise."

"That was my aim. Am I forgiven?" John held his hand out across the table, and Frank grasped it.

"Maybe," he said with a smile. "Now eat your lunch...if it's fit to eat. You've sat there preaching at me while your food got cold."

As soon as John finished his meal, they paid their checks and left.

"Where are your bags?" Frank asked.

"They're out at Grant's. My sister drove me in this morning. On her way home she dropped my things off at the ranch."

"Now what are the final plans?" Frank wanted to know as he maneuvered the car into traffic.

"Our immediate goal is to go out to Grant's and check the schedule with him. If he's free we'll make the pyramids at Teotihuacan tomorrow. I doubt that we should spend more than one day there if we want to visit the other sites we agreed on. Grant suggested that we spend tonight and tomorrow night at his place, then head toward the coast."

When the car drew up before the Bera ranch a little later, the house door slammed and Pasquelo came bounding out. "I'm going on the trip with you!" he shouted.

"You are? Your mother didn't mention it to me before I left." Frank was surprised that Margarita had given her consent. He knew she had been looking forward to his being at home during vacation.

"She didn't know it. Dad called her early this morning and she said I could go. I thought you'd never get here," he said as he approached the car. Grant advanced at a more leisurely pace.

"I see you haven't slowed him down yet," Frank teased as he put his arm around Pasquelo's shoulders.

"I've given up on that. I think it will be easier if I adapt to him. How is Señora Marquez?"

"Busy! I suppose she wrote you about Gallo."

"A rooster? No, what about it?"

"Gallo's a baby...a foundling left at the hotel."

"Pasquelo, did you know about it?"

"Yes, Mamá did tell me, but I forgot to mention it. I was getting ready for the game with Trujillo High, and it slipped my mind."

"That boy...I don't know if he is going to turn into a fish or a baseball! If he isn't practicing his breast stroke, he's slamming away at a ball. Now...tell me about this baby."

"No one knows who deserted him. I was up late

46

walking and found him on the hotel porch. I took him home, at least as far as Señora Marquez' place...and enlisted her help."

"And she still has him?"

"He's a member of the family now!"

"Well, I hope she soon finds someone to take him off her hands. He must be quite a burden."

"I don't know. In some ways it's been good for her. I'm not sure how she would have adjusted to Pasquelo's absence if she hadn't had him."

"Perhaps you're right. But come, let's get your bags...."

"We're not going to upset your routine. We'll just sleep in the station wagon."

Grant was indignant. "You'll sleep in the house like civilized men!" He whistled, and two boys came running.

"Lazaro and Ed...help Pasquelo get these bags in. Gladice will tell you where to put them. And Frank, there's room in the garage for your car. Better get it under shelter...and lock it."

The guests were aroused before daylight the next morning by whispered conversation coming from the patio. They arose and found Grant and Pasquelo busy with their work.

"I see you have him in training," Frank said when he joined them at the chicken run.

"Yes, he works around the place like all the boys I've had here. He earns his spending money this way and learns the value of a peso. He's quite a boy, Frank. You don't suppose his mother would consider my adopting him, do you?"

"Not a chance! She deeply appreciates what you're doing for him, but he's her life. Now, isn't there something John and I can do to help?"

"No, everything is on schedule. If Manuela is as efficient in the kitchen we'll soon be on our way. I told her last night that we wanted an early breakfast but chances are she is moving at her usual unhurried pace."

The cook was more alert than Grant had predicted; the morning meal was on the table when they entered the dining room. Soon the men were loading the station wagon and on the road.

"I've been to Teotihuacan a dozen times, but I'm as eager to make this trip as if I had never seen it," John said. "It's a pleasant drive, and we have good roads all the way."

"Since you've been there so often, John, you must have a lot of information about the place," Frank said.

"You have been here before, haven't you, Grant?"

"Yes, but while I *looked* at the ruins I can't say that I really *saw* them."

"I've never seen them. In fact, I was never in Mexico City until I took the village school," Frank admitted. "And I'm not proud of this negligence. I understand that people from all parts of the world come to visit these sites, while I wasn't interested enough to travel less than a hundred miles to see them. So . . . share your archaeological knowledge with us, John. Tell us what to expect."

"I doubt that anything I could say would prepare you for that. These pyramids are so awesome, so mysterious that all you can do is stand and stare in amazement. There isn't a lot of absolute knowledge about them, nor can there be, for what scientists think they know today may be refuted by tomorrow's discoveries. And it seems that many archaeologists have different theories. For instance, some date the founding of Teotihuacan at 600 B.C., some at 1500 B.C., and others as late as 100 years before Christ. According to legend it wasn't built by human hands at all but by the gods before men appeared on the earth."

"As I remember there are quite a few buildings on the site, and I read recently that more excavating has been authorized," Grant said.

"Yes, I read that, too. I wish they'd get busy on it.... I'd like to see what is uncovered next. At one time Teotihuacan was a large city. To me, the Temple of Quetzalcoatl is the most striking of the buildings, but the Pyramid of the Sun dominates the scene. It's the last of five pyramids, each one superimposed over a smaller one," John said.

"What do you mean by superimposed?" Pasquelo asked.

"Built over a smaller one, completely covering it," John explained.

"Why did they make something and then hide it?"

"Well, Pasquelo, these people looked for the end of the world at the completion of every fifty-two-year cycle. The priest watched from the top of a pyramid or a mountain for the rising sun, and when it appeared it

49

meant that they could look forward to another fifty-two years. But with the beginning of this new cycle they had to make a new start."

"Sort of a New Year's resolution?" Grant asked.

"Something like it, but there was one difference. With the new sun, all old things were destroyed and new ones made to replace them. I have read that even all clothing was burned and dishes broken. I don't know how true this is. If the housewives of that day were as attached to a plate or a bowl as my sister is to her teapot, they would have had a hard time getting dishes away from them. Actually these pyramids were mostly bases for altars. So when the new cycle began, the old altars were partially destroyed and larger, more impressive ones built over them. When we get to the top of the Pyramid of the Sun you can get an idea of the size of the ancient city. But you can't see all of it, for the greater part is hidden under fields and orchards."

"They let them make farms over the ruins?" Pasquelo asked.

"The fields were here long before anyone knew of the ruins. It's been less than a hundred years since the first excavations were made.

"We stop at the ticket window, Frank, then drive over there to park. We can get a guide book at the museum, and since you fellows haven't been here before, let's take time to go through it."

Frank followed directions, and they were soon studying the displays. Pasquelo lagged behind, reading even the lengthy explanations.

50

"Can we come back tomorrow?" he asked, when urged to hurry.

"No, we don't have time," Grant told him. "Do you have to linger over those artifacts so long?"

"If I don't learn about them, why come? I've never been here before and I can't see all this in one day."

"I know you can't. After we return from the tour we'll come out here until you can fully satisfy your curiosity," Grant assured him. "But we can't keep the men waiting now." With that promise Pasquelo reluctantly followed his elders.

One glimpse of the Temple of Quetzalcoatl dissolved all his regrets, however. They mounted the steps to the citadel and crossed the courtyard to the rear of the rectangle. Pasquelo was eager to climb the stairs to the top of the Pyramid, but John urged him on.

"Remember what I told you about one pyramid being built over another? Here's an example of it. When the archaeologists were exploring this mound, they found that it hid one much older and more interesting. Here it is—the Temple of Quetzalcoatl."

Pasquelo stopped and stared, unable to believe his eyes. "Look at this!" he called. Grant and Frank joined him, and together they marveled at the protruding serpent heads with open mouths and exposed fangs.

"See the feathers, Pasquelo?" John asked.

"Why are there feathers on a snake?"

"Perhaps because originally they were able to fly. Our birds are descended from these. The name 'Quetzalcoatl' means 'feathered serpent.' "

"Those are hideous heads," Frank observed.

"This is all symbolic, isn't it?" Grant asked.

"Yes, this goggle-eyed chap with the fangs is, some think, the rain god. Others say he is the maize god. And with these little cubical designs around him it seems to me the latter may be right, since the squares might be taken for grains of corn. This is the only temple uncovered thus far that is shared by two gods. Perhaps the sculptor was trying to depict Christ as the God of water and air. The plumbed serpent, of course, is Quetzalcoatl, symbol of the Lord."

"You don't really believe that, do you?" Frank asked.

"Yes, I do."

"Do you honestly think that grotesque figure represents Christ?"

"It's a symbol," John repeated.

Frank shook his head. "Of all the farfetched theories!" he said. "How can you connect this fanged and feathered monster with the God you worship?"

"I don't, but the ancients did. They didn't, however, worship it as God—it was a symbol of a name, not the person of the Lord," John began, but Frank cut him off.

"It's sacrilege to use any symbol for Christ. He was the Son of God."

"He *is* the Son of God," John corrected. "And the holy Communion is a symbol which Christ himself instituted. He told his disciples 'Take, eat, this is my body.' For us it is a reminder of his supreme sacrifice. And I suppose the bird-serpent was just that to these people—a reminder, nothing more. Remember how he used the serpent as a model of himself when he told his listeners that as Moses lifted up the serpent in the wilderness he, too, would be lifted up? And as the Israelites were healed by looking at the brass snake, so men would be saved by looking to him."

"But why would he choose a snake?" Frank argued.

"There are a number of theories about that, too. One is that Christ visited this continent, and when he appeared in the air the sun shone on him in such splendor that it reminded the people of the quetzal bird in flight."

"And the snake?"

"Many of us believe that the early settlers on the continent were Israelites. While they were slaves in Egypt, the snake was a symbol of divine authority, so these figures may well have their origin in that historical arena."

"Didn't the Greeks—or was it the Romans—believe that the snake had healing powers because it renewed itself each year by shedding its skin?" Grant asked.

"I think you're right. And coming to the present, don't look now, but to our left there's a United States army officer in that group of tourists. He's wearing the caduceus, which signifies that he's in the Medical Corps."

In spite of John's caution the three turned involuntarily to look at the stranger. As if conscious of being discussed, the man glanced their way.

John smiled. "Excuse us, Señor, but we were discussing the emblem on your collar."

"The caduceus? The winged staff of Hermes and the

entwined serpents is the symbol of healing. I am a doctor." He turned the pin so they could examine it more closely. John thanked him, and he moved on after his companions.

"You see, Frank, we're still using the symbol today—not because we think it has healing powers but to distinguish the person who might help us if his services were needed."

"But why choose that to typify Christ?"

"One writer makes this explanation: Even though man may grovel in the dust of sin, he is capable of winging his way to heights of righteous living. Another reasons that through Christ the chasm between heaven and earth was bridged—the bird, symbol of the spirit, and the serpent, symbol of matter. In Indian legend the soul is often represented by a feather or a plume. And I might add this thought: Jesus told his disciples in Jerusalem to be as wise as serpents and as harmless as doves. I don't know that he gave the same admonition to the people here, but it's entirely possible that he did. If so, some ardent follower may have thought it might be profitable to perpetuate that advice in stone."

Pasquelo listened to John's explanation, then followed the undulating body of the serpent around the base of the pyramid. "I want to come back here, Dad," he told Grant, "but I'm going to read up on it first. I saw some books back there in the museum that I'd like to have. Will you buy them for me and take it out of my pay?"

"I think we can manage that," Grant said indulgently.

54

"Since when did you become 'Dad' to Pasquelo?" Frank asked.

"Some time ago. Several of his friends are from north of the border...he picked it up from them."

"Now, let's get back to the Street of the Dead," John suggested. "It will take us to the larger pyramids."

As they drew near the Pyramid of the Sun Pasquelo suddenly became aware of its immensity. "Look at that!" he exclaimed. The four stopped to stare at the massive temple, then approached it in silence.

"You can understand why this is called the 'City of the Gods,' can't you?" John asked at the foot of the stairway. When they reached the top they stopped for a breathing spell while looking out over the expanse below.

"What are those small roofless cubicles down there?" Frank asked.

"That's another of the mysteries surrounding this area. According to the guide we had on one tour, this was a vast religious center and it's believed that those were offices for the priests. No one really knows." They walked around the summit viewing the scene from different angles until Pasquelo reminded them that it was lunchtime.

Frank was the last to leave. "That is a sight to remember," he said when he joined his companions on the ground.

"The buildings were at one time decorated with carvings and painted in maroon, turquoise blue, and ochre while the ground around them was paved with red stucco," John commented.

"It must have been *really* awe-inspiring then," Frank said softly.

"Well, the real tour begins in the morning, doesn't it?" Pasquelo asked as Frank drove into the garage that evening. "Where will we sleep tomorrow night?"

"We'll head for the coast in the morning, but I have no idea where we'll spend the night. . .probably in some hotel along the way."

"I've never stayed in a hotel."

"Well, it won't be like home, my boy. There'll be no late night raiding of the refrigerator," Frank warned.

A small boy tugged at his sleeve. "What's this. . .a letter for me?" Frank asked. He took the envelope, tore it open, read the enclosure, and burst out laughing.

"What's so funny?" Pasquelo wanted to know.

"There was a youngster running with the boys on the plaza whom I took to be a girl. I asked your mother to try to find out more about her. Now she writes,

Dear Señor Faz:

Knowing your anxiety about the girl on the plaza I'm sending this note by Juan since he is going into the city and can deliver it personally.

I asked Henrietta to go with me when we approached the child. Such embarrassement. . .it isn't a girl at all! When we questioned the hair ribbon he took off his trousers to prove he is a boy. So now you can go on your trip with an easy mind.

Frank chuckled as he returned the note to its envelope. "That should teach me to mind my own business!" he said.

Chapter 6

Grant left before daylight the next morning to deliver an order of eggs. While he was gone Frank and John rearranged their luggage to make room for the extra suitcases.

"Will we have space for my guitar?" Pasquelo asked.

"Certainly. With our tents and bedrolls stashed on top we'll have room for anything you need to take. Did you pack those comfortable shoes Señor Bera mentioned?" Frank asked.

"Yes, sir, they're in my bag."

"Well...don't forget anything. We won't be back this way for a month or more."

When Grant returned he changed clothes and declared himself ready to travel. Pasquelo crossed the patio with a large basket which he balanced carefully.

"What's that?" Grant asked. "You're carrying it as if it were a case of over-ripe eggs."

"Sandwiches and a jar of chocolate milk. I don't want to spill any of it."

"You won't need that, Pasquelo. We'll stop at a restaurant at noon," John told him.

"I'll be hungry long before then, Señor Acosta."

"If I know you, you're already hungry."

"Now that you mention it, I am. Guess I'll have a sandwich!" And he delved into the basket.

"If everything is stowed we'll move off. I hope we aren't leaving any suitcases behind."

"All set, Frank. Let's go."

Frank hesitated. "As I understand last night's agreement, we're leaving El Tajin for a later tour. Am I right?"

"You are. It will take more time than we have—at least more than I have," John said. "I almost wish I had turned down that tutoring job, but Judge Dias was insistent . . . and who knows when I'll need the law on my side!"

"Well, which way shall it be?" Frank asked as he started the motor.

John opened the atlas and spread the map out. "I was looking at this last night. Since we're skipping El Tajin and Zempoala we won't need to hurry to the coast. Let's take a look at Cholula; the pyramid there covers more space than those of Egypt. Then let's go on to Pueblo. I'd like to pick up some tiles there. We've bought a place in the city and will need some for the garden walks. We can play it by ear from there, with Vera Cruz as our goal."

"Cholula, here we come!" Frank said and backed the car into the road.

———————

"If we're going to camp out tonight we'd better begin looking for a place to pitch our tents," John suggested later in the week.

"I'll watch for one near the water," Pasquelo

suggested. "There...no, somebody's put a shack up behind those palms."

"That seems to be a likely spot just ahead...don't you think? And I saw a village a short distance back where we can replenish our food supply," Grant said.

John slowed the car so they could get a better look at the spot. "Seems to be ideal," he announced. "We evidently have this part of the beach to ourselves, so let's get into our swim trunks and dive in."

Refreshed, they left the water, put up tents, and built a fire. Grant and Pasquelo were taking their turn at the cooking and soon had supper sizzling over the coals. The moon rose and the stars came out while they were eating. When they had finished their meal and tidied the campsite each made a comfortable seat for himself in the sand. Only Frank seemed restless. At last he spoke. "John, you're a very disturbing fellow to be around...disturbing, puzzling, and irritating. You weren't always like this."

"Me? Irritating? And all the time I thought I was a rather agreeable chap. What have I done?"

"It's that religion of yours! You have talked all week of Christ's appearance on this continent as though it's an established fact."

"To me it is."

"What proof do you have? And what would be the point? According to the Bible he was in another part of the world, then left the affairs of the church in Peter's hands."

"What about the people here? Neither Peter nor any

of the other apostles ever visited them to tell them of Christ."

"Well, it's ridiculous to believe that he kept popping up in various places. It robs him of his divinity."

John stripped the leaves from a twig he had torn from a nearby tree as he pondered his reply. When he spoke it was with care and consideration. "I don't quite follow your thinking, Frank. It seems to me that his coming here and visiting other areas with his gospel would enhance his God-like qualities. If God is unchangeable—and we know that he is—and if he loves all of his creatures equally—as we believe—would he confine his ministry to the people in only one part of the world, or in one age?"

"Are you inferring that he appeared in various places?" Frank demanded.

"I don't know where or how many areas he visited, but I do believe he was here. He told his followers in Jerusalem that he was sent only to those of the house of Israel, and since these people were of that stock it was only natural that he came to them."

"Now you see, John, how absolutely sure you are of your belief? That's what is so irritating."

"If I wasn't sure I would never have joined the church."

"And where did you get the idea that these people were Israelites?"

"The Book of Mormon is explicit on that."

"Well, that may be conclusive proof to you, but since I don't accept the book it means nothing to me," Frank said.

"Oh, there's other outside evidence," John began, but before he could present it a band of strolling singers approached with their guitars, and it was impossible to talk above their music. When they finally left the campers got ready for bed...all except Frank. He sauntered down to the beach and walked its sandy length. John's face wore a disturbed look as he watched from his sleeping bag. His friend paced slowly, halting sometimes to look out across the water, then continued his thoughtful walk.

They were late in starting the next morning, for the musicians returned bringing breakfast with them—a long string of fish.

"José will be here in a moment with the tortillas," one of them said as the group took over the cooking. After all had eaten and cleaned the campsite, the travelers loaded the station wagon and drove off with Pasquelo hanging out the window waving and shouting "Adios" to his new acquaintances.

"What's the next stop?" Frank asked.

"This is just a thought, but why not cut out some of the smaller sites and head for Yucatan? From the markings on this map it looks as though we could spend the rest of our lives visiting ruins and still not cover them all."

"I'm in favor of that, Grant. Let's go on to Chichen Itza now and plan to see the ones we skip at another time," John suggested.

"I'm with you on that," Frank agreed. "I think we were a bit too ambitious when we charted this tour.

61

John, you're the navigator—point my nose in the right direction."

"Just follow the highway, Frank."

It was a long drive, relieved only by a stop in some village or town. Pasquelo's greatest thrill was ferrying across the Usumacinta River. He ran from one side of the boat to the other and from the lower deck to the upper level.

"You're right." He paused and then added, "You know, I've never seen a boy to whom male companionship seemed so necessary. I suppose it's because he and his father were so close. I've become so accustomed to having him with me that I dread to think of the day when he'll leave. I can appreciate how much his mother misses him."

"Yes, it was a major adjustment for her, but I know that she's grateful he's getting the education she wanted for him but couldn't afford."

"Does she have a regular income, Frank?"

"I don't know. Her husband may have left her an annuity, but if he did it's small. She has a farm that someone works on shares and the garden there in the village. And she sews for some of the women in Alhaja and nearby pueblos."

At this point Pasquelo dashed up and slipped his hand through the crook in Grant's arm. "Dad, this is almost the best part of the whole trip!" he said.

Chapter 7

Frank parked the car while Grant and John bought tickets for entrance to the Chichen site. As they followed the crowd through the gate the men were engrossed with Pasquelo's efforts to stow fruit about his person, apparently in anticipation of possible periods of famine. They surrendered their tickets and for the first time looked up to see the Temple of Kukulcan looming before them.

"I don't believe it!" Grant exclaimed. "I simply don't believe it!"

"It's more impressive than the Pyramid of the Sun, isn't it?" John asked.

"Is it real?" Pasquelo was awestruck.

"Very real...and very substantial," John assured him. "You're looking at the Temple of Kukulcan, the god known in the other parts of the country as Quetzalcoatl."

"Why does my guide book call it El Castillo?"

"One explanation is that when the Spaniards saw it they thought it was a fortification and called it 'The Castle.' That may not be so, but it's one theory."

Pasquelo moved on, and the men followed. At the base of the pyramid he met a small Indian boy and lost a race to the top. He waited there for the rest of his party, but the little boy ran down again and offered a rubber-tipped cane he carried to some women who were hesitant about climbing the stairs. Pasquelo watched the youngster as he sprinted up again.

"Why did you give the lady your cane?" he asked.

"Maybe she will give me a peso when she comes down."

"Will you get your cane back?"

"Sure. Then I'll offer it to someone else. Some days I get a lot of pesos that way."

Tourists were entering and leaving the small temple that crowned El Castillo, so Pasquelo followed those going in. The men were trailing behind, and he reappeared before they got halfway down.

"There's nothing to see down there," he told them.

"Well, since we're here we'll go on down, if for nothing more than to say we've seen it," Grant said.

"Don't wander off, Pasquelo," John cautioned. "We'll go to the Sacred Well when we come back."

Pasquelo waited impatiently at the top of the underground stairway. "Why is it called the Sacred Well?" he asked as soon as John reappeared.

"Because the people once believed that the rain god lived at the bottom of this *cenote*. During periods of drought they concluded that he was angry about something and to appease him they would toss their most beautiful girls into the water to become his brides."

"You're trying to fool me!" Pasquelo charged.

"No, it's a fact. Wait a minute, let's help this lady down, then I'll tell you about it on our way over."

"May we give you a hand?" John asked.

The elderly woman (who had been backing down the stairs) looked up. "I can't bear to look down," she explained. "I can't even climb a three-foot ladder at home, so I don't know why I thought I could go halfway to heaven in Mexico!"

"Don't look at the ground," John advised. "Just watch where you put your feet, take one step at a time, and forget how many others you have ahead of you." Continuing to talk, John dissolved her fears and soon steadied her at the base of the pyramid. She thanked him profusely and joined her friends who had lacked her courage.

"Now tell me about the well," Pasquelo urged. "Who dug it?"

"No one dug it. Perhaps that's why it was held in reverence. You see, this area has few surface rivers, and the land would really suffer if it wasn't for these *cenotes*. The soil in this area has a limestone base, so the streams eat through it rapidly and form these pockets of moisture underground. Children were chosen in infancy to be the sacrificial offerings to the rain god."

"When were they old enough for this doubtful honor?" Grant asked.

"I really don't know. They are always referred to as 'maidens,' so I presume they were in their teens. That's supposition, of course; I doubt anyone can be sure. It makes a good story for guides to tell tourists...about a lovely girl dressed as a bride loaded with jewels, being led to the well by the priests in their rich robes and elaborate headdresses, while the drums throbbed and whistles screeched. It must have been enough to frighten the poor girl to death before she got to the pool."

"Did they kill her before they threw her in?" Pasquelo asked as they paused at the brink of the well.

"I believe the victim was drugged and loaded with gifts for the god. Then, after a prayerful chant, she was tossed in."

"What if these girls didn't drown right away?" Pasquelo wondered.

"In that event they were drawn to the surface again. They were believed to have talked with Chac, the rain god, while they were down there. If they gave the priests a favorable report and a satisfactory prophecy for the coming year they were allowed to live. But if the girl was honest and confessed that she had had no communication with the god, they tossed her in again and left her there to die."

"People sure were mean then!" Pasquelo observed.

The luggage had been securely stowed and everyone comfortably seated. Grant was driving with Pasquelo beside him. "Shall we follow the coastline again on our return?" he asked.

"Let's do. That has been the most beautiful part of the trip thus far," John said.

"And we'll stop at Campeche for some more of those good shrimp. Maybe I was just particularly hungry the night we were there, but I don't think I ever ate a better meal," Grant said.

"And, Dad, we can ride the ferry again!" Pasquelo added.

"Let's see what the book says about Palenque," Frank suggested. He turned to the index. "I'm glad we decided to skip all but the important sites."

"All of them are important," John corrected him. "It's just that some have received more publicity than others, and some haven't been developed enough to make them interesting to the general public. There are some we *must* see, of course—Palenque, Monte Albán, Mitla, Xochicalco. And I'd like to spend a day or two in the city of Oaxaca."

"I'll be ready for the road home after that," Frank said. "How about you, Grant?"

"Yes...I'm beginning to miss Manuela's cooking, off-schedule though it is!"

"I'm glad that's settled." Frank closed the book. "I didn't want to suggest it, but I'm getting tired of hotel beds and meals. There's too much vibration for reading en route, so why don't you tell us something about Palenque, John? According to that article I was just reading it existed before the time of Christ."

"Yes, it belongs to the old Mayan Empire. The main interest there for most people is the Temple of the Inscriptions. It takes its name from three stone panels covered with hieroglyphics. One of Mexico's well known archaeologists was studying the Temple one day and noted a slab in the floor with two rows of circular holes spaced at regular intervals. He reasoned that the slab could be raised by using these perforations as finger holds, and he was right. The stone came up, but all he found was a stairway filled with rocks and gravel. He and his assistants cleared twenty-three steps that season and had to leave the job where it was during the rainy period. Working about three months for each of the next three years, they dug down about seventy-three feet below the temple floor only to find a rubble-filled hall. After clearing this out their first discovery was a box containing a few clay dishes and some jewelry, not enough to justify all the trouble it took to hide them. They cleaned out that part of the room, and at the foot of a large slab they found, leaning against the wall, a grave with the bones of five males and one female, believed to be teen-agers. No doubt they had been sacrificed to serve someone of importance in afterlife."

"The kids got it again!" Pasquelo observed.

"Yes, but remember, these ancients sacrificed only their very best."

"I'll bet the victims would rather have been second best."

"I'm sure they would. Well . . . the archaeologist was still unsatisfied with his finding and began searching further. While shining his flashlight around the base of this slab he saw a crack in the wall. The stone was removed revealing another short flight of steps that led down into a long, narrow chamber. It must have been an eerie experience, for water seepage had left limestone deposits that hung in long crystals from ceiling to floor. Think how these men must have felt when they stepped into a room that had been closed for over a thousand years! The space was almost filled by a huge stone coffin with a richly engraved top. This was lifted out, revealing another slab which had been cut to fit securely into the coffin below. This was raised. Inside the casket lay the skeleton of a man, evidently a king or a priest. There were rings on every finger, and bracelets covered both arms. The death mask was a jade mosaic. The inside of the tomb had been painted red and the body had, at death, been wrapped in a red robe. This had decayed, of course, but the coloring matter had dyed the bones."

"Who could have been great enough to merit such a burial?" Frank wondered.

"That is one of Mexico's many mysteries. I often think as I read of this that when the people had performed the last rites for this person, sealed the tomb, and interred the bodies of these youngsters, they never dreamed curious scientists would eventually disturb the place."

"They managed to keep it a secret for a long time. Is there any estimate of its age?" Grant asked.

"Archaeologists date it at about A.D. 625."

"Haven't I seen a model of this in the museum in Mexico City?"

"Yes, Grant, you have."

"How come you never told me about it, Dad?"

"It never occurred to me, Pasquelo."

"I want to see it when we go home."

"I think we're going to have to camp at the museum for a month," Grant told him.

"You could spend years there and not absorb it all," John said.

Chapter 8

"All right, son, the bathroom is yours," Grant said. "We want to be on the road within an hour."

Pasquelo crawled out of bed slowly, yawning and scratching his stomach.

"We'll go down and order breakfast," Frank called through the door.

Grant and Pasquelo reached the dining room just as their filled plates were being put on the table. Frank and John were almost through with their meal.

"Grant, we were talking with a tourist guide before you came down. He advised us to have a lunch packed for us. We told him we expected to do some sight-seeing on our way to Palenque, and he says that if we get off the highway we may run into a food shortage in some of the villages," Frank said.

"Good idea," Grant replied. "It would also save time. I wonder what we can get."

"This chap says we have no choice—ham and cheese sandwiches, boiled eggs, and cookies."

"Well, we won't starve on that."

Half an hour later the food was placed in the car, a supply of soft drinks stowed in the cooler, and the four took their places.

"Have a good time," the guide called as he boarded

his bus, "and if you get there first, don't eat all the shrimp in Campeche."

"These people know how to win friends for their hotel, don't they?" The men were sitting on the patio with tall glasses of fruit juice in hand.

"That they do, Grant, that they do. I've grown so accustomed to being waited on that I hate to stir. Maybe we'd better leave before we become rooted," John suggested.

"I'm ready when you are." Frank paused for a long drink. "Have you decided definitely on the route? Shall we continue down the coast to Champoton and take the highway inland or go on down to Frontera?"

"I think we'll leave the shoreline at Champoton. We won't have to wait on the ferry and we'll make better time," John said.

"How about leaving in the morning?" Grant asked.

"Good. I'll ask Mrs. Estrada if we can have an early breakfast."

Pasquelo claimed the seat beside John after they had loaded the car.

"Are there any ruins between here and Palenque?" he asked.

"No matter where you go in Mexico chances are you'll eventually come to a pyramid or a mound," John

71

assured him. "Archaeologists estimate there are at least 12,000 sites in the country. All of Middle America was densely populated at one time. No one knows who the earliest settlers were nor where they originated. Some think the continent was occupied before the great flood and an earlier civilization was destroyed then."

"Seems to me these scientists are getting fact and fancy mixed," Frank said skeptically.

"I think they may have some basis for their theory. The natives had the story of the creation, the flood, the Tower of Babel, and the confusion of tongues," John defended the theory.

"But wasn't there a regular tidal wave of Spanish priests in here with the military?" Frank asked. "No doubt the tales came from them."

"Granted the church was well represented, but the Indians who met the priests were the ones who told these stories. The natives had so many similar religious rites that the priests thought the devil must have had a hand in their education," John explained.

"I wonder if we'll ever know the real history of our land and its people," Grant mused.

"According to one legend there once was a book containing a record of their civilization beginning with the creation of the world. This was called 'The Book of God.' It was hidden in a cave and never recovered," John replied.

"Well, if it is ever found we'll have all the answers, won't we?" Grant asked.

"Rather a nebulous hope," Frank said.

"Not at all," John began, but Frank cut him short.

"No preaching, please, John. You're another one who's adept at mixing fact and fable."

"We made better time than I expected. Here we are at Palenque and it's only eleven o'clock," John said as he stopped the car under a shade tree. "Shall we have an early lunch or eat later?"

"Let's eat now," Pasquelo urged.

"We had such an early breakfast, I'm hungry," Grant said.

The sandwiches and pop were distributed, and they ate leisurely.

"It's a mystery to me why these ancient cities were not discovered sooner," Grant said, looking toward the complex of buildings spread out before them. "You wouldn't think that buildings the size of these would be easy to lose sight of."

"Most of them were completely overgrown with vegetation. And according to legend, Cholula was deliberately hidden. It's said that when the Indians learned the Spaniards destroyed their temples as fast as they found them, they determined to save Cholula. The pyramid there had been built to honor Quetzalcoatl and was doubly sacred to them. They employed teams of men and women to bring in soil from other areas to cover the pyramid. This went on day and night for months until the mound looked like a mountain. They continued to go there to worship, and when the invaders saw this they concluded that if they

73

built a church there it would be a simple matter to get the natives inside. When they began digging for the foundation of their church they found that what they thought was a mountain covered an elaborate altar."

"That was what we saw, wasn't it?" Pasquelo asked.

"Yes, we went through the church and the underground passage of the pyramid. I've often thought that other sites may have been concealed in the same way. I wish I could live to see them all uncovered. No man can hope for that though; it will take centuries at the rate we're going now. When we're through eating, let's go to the museum."

They found the place locked, but a small boy posted nearby offered to bring the caretaker. He returned a moment later with the man who unlocked the door, turned on the lights, and stepped aside as the group entered. Pasquelo was the first to comment. "Look at these people...they don't have any foreheads—just noses that end in a point at the top of their heads."

"According to some writers the people considered that a mark of beauty," John said. "Others think the disfigurement was done in order to distinguish this one tribe from others."

"How did they get them in that shape?"

"The newly born babies' heads were bound between two pieces of wood so they would grow into a point."

Pasquelo was still studying the panel when Frank walked up.

"I wish I knew what all this meant," Pasquelo said. "This looks like the profile of a man...and here's another one. And look, here's a hand, and another and another! I wonder why they all have that little dent in the palm with a circle around it?"

"Some archaeologists claim that these small depressions represent the nail wounds in the hands of Christ," John said.

"Nonsense!" Frank exclaimed.

Grant turned and asked, "What's the matter with him?"

"Oh, he's having growing pains—only he doesn't recognize them as such," John smiled. They turned back to the engraving. "Referring to the statement I just made, I don't know that I accept it, but I'm not going to eliminate the possibility until someone comes up with a better interpretation. The hand appears in many hieroglyphics. I'll confess that I don't know its significance, or that it has any. The explanation I gave you is the only one I've ever heard."

Chapter 9

"I'll take a turn at driving," Grant said when they started to leave Palenque the next day. "Monte Albán is the next site, isn't it?"

"After a brief stop at Mitla. The most unusual thing there, according to what I've read, is the decorations on the temple walls. Over a hundred thousand small cubes form its intricate patterns. From there we'll go on to Oaxaca, then Monte," John replied.

"What can we expect to find there?"

"Mystery. No one knows why a city its size—it covers approximately twenty-four square miles—was ever built on the top of a waterless mountain. It's believed that the builders shaved off the tops of neighboring heights and used the soil to fill in the low places. Dirt was also brought in from other areas and a smooth mound was raised to support the city."

"Is it possible, John, that Monte Albán was originally located where water was plentiful and raised to its present elevation by an earthquake?"

"The scientists think not, Grant."

"It seems a lot more reasonable to me than founding a city on an arid mountaintop," Frank contended.

"It is, and some day these chaps may learn that is exactly what happened."

"Can we look forward to another Chichen Itza or Teotihuacan with massive temples?"

"Not at present. There are no really tall pyramids. The main attraction here is the famous Tomb 7. Of course many mounds remain covered. There's no way of knowing what they may be hiding."

"Tell us about the tomb," Pasquelo urged.

"Well, it was under two floors, and when the slab that formed the roof of the casket was removed, the archaeologist was almost blinded by the reflection from the jewels buried there when he turned his flashlight into the grave. There were more than five hundred items of gold, silver, and precious stones. Since so many of the tombs have been rifled it's a wonder that this one escaped."

"Some very important person must have been buried there," Pasquelo observed.

"There were the skeletons of one woman and eight men, and the most important—the one wearing the jewels—was a hunchback."

"Now how do you explain that?" Frank asked.

"I don't. . . unless to the primitive mind anything that was abnormal bordered on the mysterious and the supernatural. And if the man was smart enough he could have worked on the people's superstition and elevated himself to a position of prestige and wealth; he might even have deified himself. And speaking of the mysterious, there is a small hill at Monte where I always get an eerie feeling—as though a spirit from the past were standing beside me. There is a group of small connecting cubicles on top of this hill that has an entrance but no surface exit. But below this there is a cross-shaped room, the vertical bar of which extends into a tunnel with an exit at the far end of the elevation."

"John, you have the knack of making each site more interesting than the last," Frank said appreciatively.

"Thanks. It's a fascinating study. I wish I could devote all my time to it."

They reached Oaxaca in late afternoon and decided to wait until morning to visit Monte Albán.

"Dad, there's the market! I'd like to buy a present for my mother," Pasquelo said as Grant turned into the street that led to their hotel.

"All right. Get out and wait here. I'll drive on to the hotel and be back in a few minutes."

"Let's park the car and all visit the market," John suggested.

Pasquelo stationed himself on the corner and looked over the array of merchandise crowding the streets. He became interested in a young salesman standing on the opposite corner with a tray of sweets balanced on a tripod. Flies and bees hovered over the display, but he seemed oblivious to their swarming. Noting Pasquelo's interest he lifted the container and started toward him, but when Pasquelo shook his head he settled the tray back on its support.

"This is quite a bit larger than the market at Alhaja, isn't it?" Frank asked.

78

"I'll say it is!" Pasquelo agreed. "Look at the bees over there on that tray of candy. They don't bother the boy at all. When he has a customer he just shoos them off while he makes the sale."

"What is that woman selling out of the large can?" John asked.

They watched as she took an ear of corn out of the tin of hot water, shucked it and handed it and a small swab to the purchaser. He took both, dipped the swab into a mixture of salt and red pepper, applied it to his corn, and walked off munching happily.

"I've never seen that before," Frank said.

"I haven't either...must be a custom of this area," John added.

"Another thing you don't see often is cucumber strips. They seem to sell well on hot days," Grant said.

"I don't see how a slice of wilted cucumber could be appetizing," Frank commented.

"They're not wilted, Frank. The cucumber is peeled, quartered and kept in ice water. The cucumber stays crisp. When someone stops to patronize him, the man reaches in, selects a piece, seasons it, and hands it over."

"One of the so-called charms of Mexico," John observed.

"I prefer less charm and more sanitation," Frank said. "We need stricter laws and a rigid enforcement of them."

"That would throw thousands of men and women out of work."

"I know, Grant. It's a vicious circle. If the peddlers

don't sell, they starve. If they do, they scatter disease. I think the street merchants have no need to worry, however; I doubt that we ever have such regulations."

"John, tell us what we should see here so we won't waste time in useless roaming," Grant said when they left the car at Monte Albán the next morning.

"I'm not going to give you a lot of archaeological data, but I will tell you this much. There are over two hundred sites in this area, but Monte is the best known. It's believed that man entered the valley here between seven hundred and three hundred years before Christ. Now let's go over this way."

Pasquelo ran ahead, then came back to ask, "What's that over there?"

"That's the ball court. I've never been able to decide for myself if the game was part of a religious ritual or merely a sport. Some people claim that the captain of the losing team had to submit to being beheaded by the leader of the victors. To him, I'm sure, it was anything but sport. Another opinion is that the defeated ones had to forfeit only their clothes."

"Where is the tomb you told us about?"

"Over this way, Pasquelo. We'll see it in a moment. There's something in this area I want you to see first. This was pointed out to me by a missionary, otherwise I doubt that I would have given it a second thought." They stopped before a platform which had been badly damaged by the elements or vandals. The steps needed repair, the roof was gone, and the supporting pillars were broken off above the base.

"Pasquelo, count the steps as you mount them."

He obeyed, counting as he climbed.

"There are thirty-three," he announced from the top.

"Now count the broken pillars."

"There are twelve."

Grant caught the implication at once. "You think this points to the thirty-three years of Christ's life and his twelve disciples?"

"I don't know, but it's something to think about."

They lingered for a moment, then walked on slowly.

"I'm hot and thirsty, and I know you must be too," John said as they crossed the plaza. "I saw a woman over the way sitting by a portable ice chest.... Maybe she has some liquid refreshment." And John led them to the spot.

"Well, this is our last stop before we head for home, isn't it?" Frank said at the entrance to the ruins at Xochicalco. "I'm glad. In fact, to be honest with you I could pass this one by."

"This is one of the most interesting of all the sites," John assured him. "At one time it was a cultural center. Young men were sent here to train for the priesthood. Look at the carvings on the walls. They're almost completely covered. Now over here beyond the stairway is an engraving that fascinates me, and I've never had anyone explain it to my satisfaction although I've read many books on the subject. Some say that it has to do with the calendar, but I wonder. I want you to notice particularly this rectangle...."

"That looks like a box with a rope tied around it," Pasquelo interrupted.

"And here is a hand holding the other end of the rope," John continued, "and another hand is extended over the rectangle, or box, as though in blessing."

"I don't think so," Pasquelo disagreed. "I'll bet there's treasure in the box and the hand is guarding it. I saw a movie like that once. The villain was always trying to open the box, but every time he tried to raise the lid a hand came out and just stayed there in the air over the box. No matter how hard he tried he couldn't budge it. Hey, look at these two circles with holes in the middle. When I was a kid that's the way I drew eyes."

"You took the words right out of my mouth," John said.

Pasquelo continued to study the carving. He started to speak, then stopped. Grant, who had been watching, saw him reach out and trace the sculpture with his finger.

Chapter 10

"There's no need for you fellows to rush off. You have plenty of time to rest up, and you might as well spend it here. After some of the meals we had on the trip I'm sure you can eat Manuela's cooking for a while. Let's sit on the porch...she's going to bring out some lemonade in a few minutes," Grant invited.

"You've just talked us into it," Frank replied.

"Professor Faz and I used to have lemonade every evening after I'd finished my lessons," Pasquelo remembered. "By the way...how am I going to get my present to Mamá?"

"Why not go home with me? There's time for a visit with her before school starts," Frank said.

"That's a good idea, but remember, she's had peace and quiet for some time—she'll need a while to get used to your noise again," Grant cautioned.

The travelers relaxed for two days then declared they must leave. Frank dropped John at his gate, saying, "I won't come in because I'll stay too long, and I want to get back to the village before dark. It's been a wonderful vacation, and I'd like to plan a similar one for next year. And just because you have no further excuse for deluging me with quotations from the Book of Mormon, don't quit writing."

"I'm sorry I played that trick on you, Frank. I just wanted you to know what it was all about."

"Well, if you wanted me to read the book why didn't you say so? Give me a copy, and I'll read it."

"You will?"

"Listen, I read every word in Father Fidel's Bible and Lola's prayer book. After that I think I can take on your Mormon Scripture."

For a moment John was stunned with surprise, then dashed into the house and came out with the book.

"Don't stand there looking as though a miracle had happened," Frank teased. "I merely said I'd read it . . . not accept it."

"That's all I ask," John replied quietly.

"I won't say when, but I'll read every word of it. Now we'll be off . . . but keep in touch. And since you're going to live here in the city, there's no reason why you can't come see us frequently." Frank waved good-bye and began the trip home.

"I'll be glad to see my mother," Pasquelo confessed. "I wish she'd move to Mexico City."

"That, I think, is an impossibility. Everything she has, except you, is in the valley."

Frank stopped speaking and listened carefully. "Do you hear a knocking in the engine, Pasquelo? Wouldn't it be the limit if, after all the trouble-free driving we've done, the car began acting up now?"

"It sounds like little rocks rolling around in a tin can," Pasquelo observed.

"I'm going to pull over into the open space ahead and see if I can locate the trouble."

As soon as they were off the highway Frank raised the hood and looked under it.

"Hand me the flashlight, Pasquelo. . . . Now, direct the ray where my hand is. I think I see what's causing the noise."

Frank worked for an hour with Pasquelo holding the light and supplying tools as they were called for.

"Well, that's all I can do," Frank said, lowering the hood. "I hope this gets us home. We'll have to drive slowly. It's going to be dark before we get to the valley."

After four more stops to work on the car, Frank drove into his own yard at two o'clock. Pasquelo wanted to arouse his mother to present his gift, but Frank persuaded him to wait until morning.

He was awakened by the ringing of church bells. The sun hadn't been up long enough to dispel the early morning chill, so he settled comfortably back on his pillows and dozed off, half conscious of a low rippling sound. It took a moment for him to get oriented, then he recognized the whisper of the wind in the corn. He breathed deeply, relishing both the sound and the fragrance.

He soon heard the plodding feet of the cattle as they passed the house on their way to pasturage on the hill and the braying of donkeys at opposite ends of the village.

Frank sat up and saw that Pasquelo had already left his hammock. He went to the back door and met the boy coming in with a large ripe tomato in hand.

"I came in to get some salt," he said. "You should see

the garden. We have the biggest tomatoes I've ever seen." Frank handed him the salt shaker. Pasquelo sat down, moistened an area of the fruit with his tongue, dusted it with salt, and began to eat. He sighed with satisfaction when he had finished.

"I think I'll go over and wake Mamá," he said.

"Do that, and ask her if she can feed two hungry men this morning."

Pasquelo dashed out, and a moment later the glad cries from the house next door told Frank that Pasquelo had announced his arrival.

A little later Margarita called her neighbor over for breakfast. "I had forgotten how active my son is. He's inspected every inch of the house and yard and now he's doing the village!"

"I know. He raided your tomato patch before daylight."

"You're to come over for supper, Señor Faz. We're going to have a real celebration," Margarita informed him as he left.

She began cooking for the evening meal before the breakfast dishes were washed, and when she called Frank in for supper, the table was lavishly spread. Pasquela ate until he could hold no more.

"Now tell us about the trip, Señor Faz. We kept the postcards you sent. I had no idea there were such places in Mexico. My husband and I visited Teotihuacan on our honeymoon, but judging from the pictures I would say there have been many changes since then."

Frank and Pasquelo spent several hours telling about

their tour, and it was dark when Frank arose to leave. "I need a walk after that meal," he said. "I'll go up and talk to Henry and Henrietta for a while."

"Did you get your car fixed?"

"No, Pasquelo. Bonificio pulled it down to his place to work on it. He thinks he'll have it running tomorrow. . . . Thanks for the supper, Señora Marquez; it was delicious."

Frank took his walk, stopped for a while at the hotel, then returned home. Later Pasquelo knocked.

"Are you busy?"

"Not particularly, Pasquelo. I thought I might begin charting next term's classwork."

"May I see that book John gave you?"

"Yes, indeed. Have a chair and start in."

But Pasquelo preferred the floor. He took the Book of Mormon to a spot near the lamp, and for some time there was little sound in the room except for the scratch of Frank's pen and the rustle of paper as Pasquelo turned a page. Both were startled when Margarita called Pasquelo home.

"I'll see you tomorrow," he promised as he left.

Frank stretched his arms over his head and yawned. He took the book Pasquelo had put aside, opened it at the beginning, and read, "I, Nephi, having been born of goodly parents. . ."

"That's quaint," he said to himself, "but an interesting introduction." He read the phrase. "Well, it's reassuring to know that you come of good stock. I can say the same for myself, Nephi, old chap." He read for thirty minutes, then laid the book down. "It's going to be heavy going, and I vowed I wouldn't skip a word." He stepped out onto his porch and decided to take another walk. He passed through his gate and up the road to the plaza. He hadn't realized before how very quiet the town was. The houses were dark, the streets and lanes almost deserted. Only an occasional intoxicated villager staggered over the cobblestones homeward bound. "I'd better get some rest," he told himself, and a half hour later he had joined his fellow townsmen in sleep.

The next night as he continued his work on the school program Pasquelo came in. "Care if I read some more in the book?" he asked.

"Of course not. It's there on the bed table."

Pasquelo sprawled out on the floor and began reading. "This is interesting," he commented after a while.

Frank looked up from his work. "That? Interesting? If I hadn't promised John I'd read it I'd send it back tomorrow."

"Maybe you haven't reached the best part. . . . I sort of skip around. Do you know that in one battle 230,000 men were killed? I don't know where this war was fought, but it must have been on a big battlefield."

"According to John it was fought here."

"In Mexico?"

"On this continent."

"I'll read farther and see if I can find out about that."

Frank returned to his work and Pasquelo to his reading. For a few minutes there was silence, then Pasquelo burst forth again. "It was in a land where there were lots of rivers and fountains near a hill called Cumorah. Did you ever hear of it?"

"No, it's new to me."

"One captain's name was Mormon. He hid a lot of records in this hill where the battle was fought."

Frank looked up, all attention.

"What did you say about a record?" he asked.

"This Mormon says he was commanded to keep the records from falling into the hands of the Lamanites— the bad guys—so he hid them in this hill."

"Let me see that, Pasquelo." Pasquelo handed it over but stood by, eager to finish the story. Frank wanted to pursue the account himself, but seeing the boy's impatience he made a mental note of the page and returned the book.

For a few moments Pasquelo sat looking thoughtfully into space, then asked, "Was there a lot of water at Xochicalco?"

"I don't recall seeing any."

"Do you remember the carving on the temple wall there where there was a box with a rope tied around it?"

"Yes. . . that was one of the most interesting of all the places we visited."

"Well, I've been thinking. I'll bet all those hieroglyphics tell about this record and how it was hid in the box."

"Archaeologists think the hieroglyphics have to do with dates."

"What do they know?"

"A great deal more than you or I."

Pasquelo turned back to the book. "I'm going to ask Dad to buy one for me and take it out of my pay."

"That will make John very happy," Frank commented.

"Pasquelo . . ." the call came from next door.

He arose reluctantly and put the book on the table.

"Come back tomorrow and finish your tale," Frank invited. "I'd let you take the book home with you, but I promised John I'd read it and I'll have to work on it."

"Thanks anyway . . . and thanks for letting me come over."

"Glad to have you at any time, Pasquelo."

It was too early to think of going to bed, so Frank again strolled up to the hotel. The plaza was crowded with young men and the village waifs were having a battle with the refuse from the market square. He dodged their missiles and called a warning as he walked on. Henry was leaning across the counter smoking. He straightened up as Frank entered.

"Come in, come in, Professor. What will it be—a beer, a coke, or a cup of coffee?"

"Nothing, thank you, Henry."

"Oh, come, now. On the house?"

"No, I was just restless and decided to get out for a while." He sat at one of the empty tables and stared into the street. Henry came from behind the counter with two filled cups.

"What's the matter with you?" he asked. "You've no cause to be so gloomy. You don't have a wife to nag you; you have an interesting job, a nice home with good neighbors, and everyone likes you. So why are you so gloomy?"

"Perhaps it's because I have so little to do."

"I wish I had that complaint! It won't be long before school starts.... You'll be busy enough then."

"Speaking of school, can you tell me why those children out there don't attend—those who are old enough, that is? I wonder what their ages are."

"Impossible to say for sure—probably five to seven," Henry replied indifferently.

"I don't think there are as many there now as there were at noon."

"About half. Some have working mothers, and some have folks who just don't want to be bothered with them. They bring them to the plaza and dump them. The older ones are supposed to take care of the younger kids but they seldom do."

"Something must be done if they are to become productive adults rather than drags on society," Frank said.

"I know they should be in school, Professor, but how do you go about educating kids whose own parents reject them? The only home some of them know is the street. They wear what someone gives them or what they can steal, and they depend on the generosity of the townspeople for their food, and sometimes there isn't too much of that—generosity or food."

"It never occurred to me before, but why can't

shelter be furnished for them? Aren't the citizens of Alhaja progressive and affluent enough to support such a place?" Frank asked.

"Why should we? They aren't our kids," Henry said.

"Children shouldn't be held responsible for the delinquency of the parents. What can the future hold for such neglected youth?"

"I don't know, but I *do* know that bankruptcy is staring me in the face unless I can stop those little thieves from stealing everything not nailed down. They're smart enough to wait until the place is jumping with tourists, then they swarm in here like a colony of ants. When I have time to check I find they've cleaned me out of half my stock. There's a foxy one out there. He hasn't been in town more than a month but already he's the leader. That Anselmo is the slickest operator I've ever seen. He grabbed a lady's purse as she got off the bus one day last week. It was pure luck that Joe was on hand and retrieved it."

"Well, I suppose if you're half starved you'll resort to anything to appease your hunger. I think it's a disgrace that we've let this condition arise. I believe that if we can get responsible villagers together we can come up with a plan to correct this situation. Poor kids...what have they to look forward to if they go to sleep at night cold and hungry, knowing they can expect the same the next day?"

"What's got you so steamed up about this, Professor?"

"I don't know...perhaps seeing the care Señora Marquez gives the two she has taken into her home, and the concern Grant Bera has for those he seeks to educate."

"But these kids don't belong to us. Some of them are from other pueblos."

"Do you remember the parable of the Samaritan and the Jew?"

"Oh, yes. I'm a Christian."

"There's your answer. These are human beings. Their bodies feel hunger and cold as ours do. They're helpless to help themselves, and no one cares."

"I know you're right, Professor, but I doubt that you can change the condition."

"Why not? Can't we afford to build a shelter for these children? And the next step, after we've done that, is to get them in school. They must be taught."

"You have good ideas, I'll admit—good but impossible!"

"Why?"

"You want some reasons? For a start, how could we construct a building?"

"With adobe bricks. Perhaps Rafael, Jason, and José will supply them. I recently read of a village south of here that had erected a hospital just through the combined efforts of its residents. We have enough idle men and boys in Alhaja to get a shelter up in record time. They are required to keep the church in repair, cultivate Father Fidel's garden, and contribute time to public works. Why can't they do something for these children?"

"All right, you've got the materials and labor

donated. Where are you going to build this shelter?" Henry asked.

"Why not make it an addition to the schoolhouse?" Henrietta had joined them with her coffee.

"The very thing, Henrietta! There's plenty of room on the south side of the building. And if they're that near the school it shouldn't be too much of a problem to get them inside."

"You're both dreamers. Can you imagine what the place would be after those kids have been there a couple of nights? Take a look at the plaza when you go home, Professor, and you'll get the picture."

"They'll need supervision, of course," Henrietta conceded, "and there must be hammocks or *petates* for them to sleep on. And they'll need a place to take their meals."

"I'm going to have you locked up, Henrietta," her husband threatened. "And I may have the Professor committed, too. Where would you get the food and someone to cook it?"

"Do you know who would be perfect for the job?" Henrietta ignored Henry's question and leaned across the table in her eagerness.

"No, unless you'd take it on."

"Margarita Marquez."

"Perfect is right! You see, Henry, it takes a woman to solve our problems."

"You can't ask her to take on that responsibility without paying her, and where is the money to come from?"

"Henry Hernandez, if you don't quit thinking up

94

obstructions I'm going to bring that bunch of kids in here for a month!" Henrietta vowed.

Henry rolled his eyes in a gesture of utter despair.

"There are enough businessmen and women in town to finance this. Henry, you're the mayor, why can't you levy a small tax—just enough to cover expenses?" Henrietta asked.

"Now wait a minute! I have no authority to levy taxes. And don't you start meddling in village politics. I have enough trouble already."

"I know one way we can raise a little money. The kids meet every bus that stops here and beg, often with good results. I'll put a box here on the counter as they do in large cities when they're trying to raise money for charity. I'll ask the drivers and their passengers to contribute to our fund rather than give it to the children. I believe they'd rather do that than to have the youngsters tugging at their sleeves the minute they get off the bus," Henrietta said.

"Speaking of buses, there comes Ben with his load now." Henry arose and took his stand behind the counter while the waitresses lined up against the wall.

"Frank, let's think this through carefully. I see all sorts of possibilities. Talk to Margarita and see how she feels about taking the job provided our plan develops," Henrietta called as she joined Henry.

Frank spent a restless night. His mind was filled with plans for the plaza waifs. If only he could arouse enough interest among the villagers there would be no problem, but . . . and here he had to let the matter rest. He was awakened the next morning when Margarita and Pasquelo stepped onto his patio.

"I'll be with you in a moment," he called as he hastily dressed.

"We didn't mean to get you out of bed," Margarita apologized.

"It's high time! I was restless last night and didn't get to sleep until near morning. Come in . . . I'll make some coffee."

"Thanks—I've had mine. What I came for was to ask you about a book Pasquelo was reading over here last night. He kept me awake telling me about stories he found in it and trying to connect them with some picture writing he saw somewhere on the tour. Is this a book that he should be reading?"

"It's harmless—fanciful, but harmless," Frank assured her.

"Well, if you say. I wouldn't want him reading anything that would give him ideas like those trouble-makers at Guadalajara I've been reading about in the newspaper."

"There's really nothing in the book to influence him one way or the other."

"Well, thanks. . . . I just wanted to be sure. I'll send Lola over to get your breakfast," she called as she followed Pasquelo into their own yard through the gap in the gardenia hedge. Frank suddenly remembered that he was to discuss the proposed shelter with her and called her back.

"Wait. Do you have a minute, Margarita?"

"Of course."

"Sit down, please, while I get my coffee."

Frank talked as he moved about, briefly outlining the conversation he'd had with Henry and Henrietta Hernandez. "Would you consider taking the job if this materializes?"

"It's a wonderful plan, and I appreciate your thinking of me, but I couldn't do it. It would necessitate my being away from home during the day and a good part of the night. I wish I could, though, because I've got to make some provision for Gallo, and I need the money."

"I see. It just seemed to us that you were the only qualified person in the village."

"Mamá!" a baby voice called from the patio.

"You see what I mean. Here's Mamá, Gallo." She arose and helped him across the threshold.

"Ah, Professor, you had to make your own coffee!" Lola had trailed Gallo.

"Yes, I made it, but I can't drink it."

Lola took the cup, smelled it, and regarded its contents with a wry face. "What did you do to it?"

"I made it just as I've seen you do. I put a cup of ground coffee...."

Lola bent over in her amusement. "Yes, I use a cup to make the essence, but only a spoon of that and a cup of hot water for your drink," she explained.

"What do you do with the rest of the essence?"

"That lasts a week or longer, depending on how much you drink. Didn't you ever make coffee before?"

"Yes, but I've always used instant."

"That isn't good," Margarita said. "It has no body."

"I agree, but it's quick and simple."

"For a man alone I suppose it's the answer. Come, Gallo, we must go home and let Lola get her work done."

Chapter 11

After breakfast Frank went across the road to the schoolhouse and looked at the area he and Henrietta had considered for the shelter. He sighed, then walked on up to the hotel. A bus had pulled up in front and the passengers were pouring out. He went around to the patio entrance as Henry came through carrying a laden tray.

"You don't make a very good waiter, Henry. You're spilling things all over the floor."

"Ah!" Henry paused to balance the tray. "That Lozano! I ought to fire him."

"Where is he?"

"In jail...drunk...and the girls don't come today until noon! This is an unscheduled stop and we're simply not prepared for it! Henrietta and I are waiters, counter help, cashier, and busboy."

"Perhaps I can help. Maybe I can handle the candy and cold drinks section."

"Get in there and man the cash register!" Henry motioned with his head. Frank obeyed.

"I believe I can handle the entire counter, Henrietta. Go help Henry wait tables before he has a stroke."

She gladly relinquished her post. For the next hour there was no time for conversation. After the tourists left Henry said, "You're a real friend, Professor. We'd never have made it without your help. We didn't even have anyone to send for Margarita. We call on her when we get in a tight spot. Now that the rush is over, here comes Vincente."

"I'm glad I was here, Henry. I rather enjoyed it."

"What did Margarita think of our project?" Henrietta asked.

Frank explained her position. "She would like to take it on, because with Lola and Gallo to provide for she needs the extra money."

Henrietta rubbed her chin thoughtfully. "I wonder if she'd consider it if it were nearer her house."

"It couldn't be any nearer unless you built it in her yard," Henry said.

"Hm, yes, that's exactly what I was thinking. There she goes into the post office. I'm going to send Vincente over and ask her to join us."

The boy soon returned followed by Margarita. Henrietta launched into the subject immediately. "Margarita, you don't use that space between your house and Frank's place, do you?"

"No, why?"

"Frank has told you about hopes for a shelter for the plaza kids. If it was built in your yard do you think you could corral them?"

"I could try."

"That settles it," Henrietta said with finality.

"Do we need permission to construct the building?" Frank asked.

"Henry will talk to the jefe about it. It's always good to have him on your side. And he can recruit help.

100

Instead of lying in jail doing nothing, the lawbreakers could assist in building the shelter."

"Not so fast, Henrietta," her husband cautioned. "You aren't running the show, remember."

"Want to bet on that?" Frank asked with a wink at Henrietta.

"I have something to say on the subject," Henry said. "We four certainly can't do this alone, and if we ask the people to help—as we must—they should have a voice in where such a place should be built and who should be in charge."

"You're right," Henrietta agreed promptly. "We'll give 'em a chance to vote on it. And if anyone knows of a person more capable than Margarita or a place more appropriate than the lot next to her house, let him speak up."

"Ah, here comes Seguro. Vincente, tell Victoria that Seguro is here for his breakfast. She'd better give him oatmeal this morning." A tiny boy clutching a tin can hesitated in the door. "Go on back, Seguro. Victoria will feed you."

"What's the can for?" Frank asked.

"That's what he eats from. He brings it with him each time he comes, and before he leaves he goes to the fountain and washes it."

"How old is he?"

"Who knows? There's no way to establish the ages of these children. They're stunted physically and mentally by lack of food. Seguro may be three or four or five. He's too small to compete with the other boys

101

in securing scraps of food. In fact he was almost starved when we noticed him."

"I want to take him home with me to keep," Margarita said, looking after the child as he passed through the sunlit patio into the dimness of the rooms beyond.

"*You* want to keep him?" Henrietta said unbelievingly.

"He's so thin and has such wistful eyes," Margarita explained.

"You'd adopt all the strays if you could, wouldn't you?" Henrietta smiled at her friend.

"Isn't that what you're asking me to do?" Margarita asked.

"Yes, I suppose it is," Henrietta conceded.

"I wonder who gave the child his name...Seguro. I doubt that he has ever known security," Frank said as the boy returned, holding his tin can tightly.

Margarita called him to her. He advanced and stood near but refused to let her touch him. But when Frank held out his hand he went to him readily and sat on his knee.

"He needs a bath," Henrietta observed. "And some clothes. It's a puzzle to me how he keeps those rags on his body."

Seguro began to show signs of restlessness.

"Señora Marquez, if you're sure you want to add this child to your family we'd better start home before he decides to leave us."

As she arose to follow Frank Henrietta said, "I'll

102

send one of the boys down with some food this afternoon."

"There's no need, Henrietta. I can feed one more small one."

"You've done enough in taking in Lola and Gallo. We've been keeping Seguro alive for some time now—we can continue. Frank, we'll talk the project over with our patrons. If we approach them in the right way I believe they'll respond."

Lola was very critical of the new addition to the family. "He stinks," she said, wrinkling her nose.

"He does," Margarita admitted, "but the odor will wash off with the dirt. Gallo didn't smell so good either when he came to us. I'm going up to Señora Valdez' shop and see what material she has suitable for a small boy's clothes."

"Shall I wash him while you're gone?"

"Yes, if he'll let you."

"I doubt that he will. He seems to be afraid of women." Frank had been standing near. "Let me take both boys over to my place and bathe them at the same time."

"Gallo is clean," Lola objected. "He doesn't need a bath."

"I know, Lola, but if Seguro sees him submitting to a good scrubbing he won't be afraid to try it himself."

Frank filled a tub on his patio and after letting Gallo

103

splash and play in the water, he drew a fresh container for Seguro. Frank stripped him and lowered him into the tub and stood by as he tried to imitate Gallo's antics. He soon tired of it, however, and the teacher knelt and began soaping the dirt-encrusted body.

"Poor little tyke," he murmured, "you're so skinny I can count every rib." After the bath, he wrapped a dry towel around Seguro and returned to the Marquez home where he found Lola cutting out small trousers while Margarita stitched them up on the sewing machine.

"Did he give you any trouble, Professor?"

"He didn't like to surrender that can at first... wanted to hang on to it even while I was bathing him. See—he's still holding on to it. Do you have anything I can feed him?"

"I'll take care of him. Come, Seguro...you, too, Gallo."

"He's so thin I don't see how he gets around."

"Gallo was almost as pathetic when I first saw him. But just wait—I'll soon have him as round as an apple."

———

Frank stood at the door and looked out over the school yard filled with laughing children. The sharp clang of the bell brought them running to fall in line; then they filed into their classrooms with the teachers following. They had been back in school for a week, but were just beginning to settle down to routine. It had been a difficult time for Frank because his mind was divided between his teaching and his hopes for the shelter. He was relieved when the day was over and Genero rang the dismissal bell.

Two pupils from each room stayed late to clean up for the next day. Frank paused long enough to give them their instructions, then crossed the road home. But at a wave of Lola's hand from the Marquez yard he stopped and Margarita came to meet him.

"Henrietta wants to see you," she said.

"Then I'd better go find out what she wants." He retraced his steps to the road and went on to the hotel.

"You want to see me, Henrietta?"

"Yes, Frank. Come over here where we can talk." She took two sodas from the refrigerator and followed him to a table. "Here, cool off." She set one of the bottles before him and half emptied hers before explaining her summons.

"When Remundo was here this morning I approached him with our plan. I can't honestly say that he's enthusiastic about it and he isn't too hopeful of its success, but he's willing to go along with us. He says if we can get the materials donated he's sure he can provide laborers. With a number of fiestas coming up he says he won't have room in the jail for all the lawbreakers. He thinks though, that we should have a meeting of all the business people of the village and present the plan to them."

"He's right—we'll need their help. Will he call the meeting?"

"No, since Henry's the mayor, he sent word. . . ."

"You mean that you told the people when and where to meet." Henry set his cup of coffee on the table and looked at her.

"For the past four years, Professor, I've been elected mayor and my wife immediately takes over."

"You're too slow," Henrietta said. "I like to get things done."

"When is the meeting to be held?" Frank asked.

"Saturday morning at nine on the patio. And now we've got to get busy. Henry, the lady who had No. 6 last night said the light bulb burned out while she was reading. You'd better have Vincente replace it right away."

Chapter 12

The hotel patio was crowded Saturday morning. Henry turned the meeting over to Frank as soon as he had explained the purpose of the gathering. Not that it was necessary, for the reason for their coming together had been well publicized.

"I wonder if any of us really appreciate our great country," Frank began. "I wonder how many of us are proud of our Indian-Spanish ancestry. We Mexicans have inherited the best of two great nations. No other land can boast of more beauty; no other land has such a history; no other land deserves more to be loved and cherished. And nestled in the heart of it is our village. Alhaja has been rightly named 'the Jewel,' for when we look down from the mountaintop into the valley it resembles a giant fire opal. The colorful houses and bright gardens gleam like a precious stone."

A round of applause forced him to pause. Then he continued, "But like many a gem there is a flaw in its loveliness. I am referring to the neglected or abandoned children who make the plaza their home during the day and bed down at night wherever they can find any semblance of shelter. These pathetic youngsters haunt every passerby with cries—and even demands—for money, and now I am told they have even resorted to purse-snatching. It's frightening when you stop to think that we are nurturing right here in our village a group of potential bandits. What are we going to do with them?"

"Take 'em across the border to Texas," someone suggested. There was a ripple of laughter.

"Texas doesn't need our delinquents. It has enough of its own. These boys are Mexican—they are ours, and whether we like it or not, they're our problem."

"They're not mine. I've got seven of my own—all I can feed," someone called out from the audience.

Frank saw Father Fidel come in and take a back seat. Seeing the priest gave him an idea; he decided to approach the matter from another angle, since he seemingly had made little impression thus far.

"Pete, are you a Christian?" he asked.

The man singled out hestitated, squirmed, and then said, "Of course. I go to mass regularly and to confession twice a year."

"And what is a Christian?"

There was silence for a moment, then the priest spoke, " 'Christian' was the name given the followers of Christ."

"How did they merit the name, Father?"

The priest was disconcerted at first by the probing question, then replied, "Why, by obeying Christ's commands."

"Thank you, Father. There you have it, Pete. A Christian takes orders from Christ, and one of them is 'Bear ye one another's burdens.' This might be followed with another scripture, 'Inasmuch as ye have done it to one of the least of these...ye have done it unto me.' If Christ were here now, would you let him go hungry or sleep in an old car?"

"Say, Frank, are you a teacher or a preacher?" one of the men called out.

"I hope I'm a humanitarian," he replied. "Now I've tried to appeal to you people in two ways and apparently have failed in both. This time I'm going to touch your wallets.

"Henry, how much do you lose to these youngsters in the course of a year?"

"I don't know.... I've never tried to total it. Some days I don't suppose they get away with more than four or five pesos. On others it will run ten... twenty... perhaps more."

"Well, let's say an average of five pesos a day. In a year's time that's over 1,800 pesos."

"Caramba! No wonder I'm going broke!"

"Are you sure of that?" asked Señora Ruiz who had a candy store.

"Figure it for yourself. What do you think your losses run?"

"Less than that—but far too much."

Frank could see other shopkeepers silently estimating their losses, and he felt that he had at last struck home.

"Henry, are you willing to contribute to maintaining a shelter for these boys provided we keep them away from the hotel?"

"If you can fence them in somewhere so they won't steal from me I'm willing to help pay for the pen."

"We're going to get them in school where we can

keep an eye on them in daytime and prepare them for something else besides begging."

"In school? How are you going to do that?"

"It must be done. The shelter is only the first step," Frank replied. "Listen, I love Mexico. It's my country and I want to see it take its place beside other great nations of the world. But we cannot hope to make it succeed until an education is made possible for all of its people. Now I'm not going to ask for a commitment yet. Go home and think this over and decide how much it's worth to you to get these children off the streets and into the classroom. You might think about this, too. If we permit purse-snatchers to meet our buses, the operators of the tourist routes are going to find other stopping places. Can we afford to lose the money they bring in? Now let's get together this time next week with a decision."

Most of the group hurried off to their places of business but some lingered to discuss the plan further.

"We've never done anything like this before and we've always gotten along all right," Albert Orosco argued.

"I'm sure you have, Al, but how about those boys? How have they fared?"

"You're new to the village, Frank. You don't understand us. We let every one alone to attend to his own affairs."

"And what I've been trying to tell you, Al, is that these children are our affair. Our own safety depends on lifting them to a higher standard of living. You say you're doing well, and I'm sure you are, for your mill is

110

never idle. Your children are well dressed and well fed, are being well educated. Some day Anselmo will wonder why he couldn't have had the same advantages."

"I'll tell him why! It's because he had a no-good mother and a rat for a father. My kids are getting the better things of life because I've worked to provide them."

"Anselmo may want the same for his children some day. He may demand it, and if he doesn't get it he may take it. Al, we can't afford to have another revolution, but when we neglect the unfortunate we sow the seeds of civil war."

Al sat looking at him sullenly. "I just don't get it, Frank. What got you off on this kick?"

"I'm not sure, but I know I'm very serious about getting these children into the classroom during the day and under adequate shelter at night. When I go to bed I want to know that they aren't hungry and shivering with cold."

"That's something else you have to figure in this deal—food and clothes."

"I know. You might contribute regularly a certain amount of *masa* from your mill. There are enough prosperous people in the village to supply all the needs without putting a burden on anyone."

Frustrated and angry, Al arose and walked over to the counter to pay for his soda.

"Think it over for a few days, Al," Frank advised. "You'll see the logic in it."

"Well, Professor, did you accomplish anything?" Henry asked as he eased his bulk across the counter and lit a cigarette.

"I'm not sure, Henry. What do you think?"

"Hard to tell, but I have an idea that more than one merchant is sitting down right now with pencil and paper trying to tally his losses. When you come right down to it, it would be cheaper to keep those kids in school."

During the week Frank made several attempts to read the book John had given him. But his thoughts were on the homeless children, and he spent every evening on the plaza, trying to talk with them, watching until sleep drove them to empty doorways or an empty car. He could hardly wait for the next meeting. There was a record turnout on Saturday when he arose to make his second appeal for the unfortunate.

"I hope you have all given serious consideration to the matter we discussed last week," was his opening remark.

"What will it cost us?"

"How much is it worth to you, Victor?"

"That's a difficult question, Frank. I'm willing to help get these kids housed. I'll furnish the paint you need inside and out and the labor to apply it."

"Splendid, Victor! Thank you. Now who's next on the donor list?"

"My brother and I will supply half the adobes if the Dominguez boys will furnish the other half and we can get some help in preparing the clay."

Other offers followed, especially after Henrietta arose and made her speech. "If a young widow who has to work for her living can take in two homeless babies and a teen-age girl, a village of five hundred should be able to take care of eight or ten children. Let's make Margarita our model."

The committees were appointed, the site and the supervisor approved.

"Margarita's a brave woman," Señora Valdez said. "Imagine having a dozen boys running all over the place."

Frank crossed the road to his own house just as Grant's car glided past him and stopped before the Marquez home. Pasquelo darted out of the house and ran to meet him.

"Hey, Dad, I've been helping make brick. Come see what we've done."

"Just a minute, Pasquelo, I want to talk to Frank." He turned to his friend. "I've been half hoping this venture would fail ever since I first heard of it. It seems to me that this is too much of a burden to put on Señora Marquez."

"I don't think so, Grant. I'll be near if the boys get unruly. I'll admit that the two babies require a lot of care, but the others can take care of themselves and help her as well. They have to have supervision, and she seems the logical choice. Besides, she can use the small salary this venture will pay."

"What is the salary?"

"We haven't settled that yet. A lot depends on how well the villagers continue to support us. The project is being developed entirely by volunteer labor...well, not always volunteer. When our local *jefe* or the state police arrest an offender he's put to work on the building. If his guilt is drunkenness—and it usually is—he's sobered up in jail and given a sentence of either building or gardening. I might add that it takes quite awhile to work off the fine."

"I hope you're going to put up a more substantial kitchen," Grant observed. "If that cane and thatch affair ever caught fire with Margarita in it, it could be tragic."

"We're building a real kitchen. It will be attached to the dormitory."

"She isn't going to do the cooking too, I hope."

"Oh, no, we will have three or four women helping with the manual labor. Then we have Lola. She's really my housekeeper, but there's so little to do in my Spartan ménage that she spends most of her time over here. She looks on this as high adventure."

"I hope it proves nothing worse."

"You aren't very optimistic!"

"I don't want to discourage you, Frank, but I think you're taking a big chance."

"Grant, if you had a son out there wouldn't you want someone to take a chance?"

114

"Of course. And you're right...you must try. I'm inclined to express my opinion too freely when it concerns someone I care about. Now I'd better say 'good-bye' to Margarita, gather my boy, and be off."

"Here he comes now." Frank indicated the approach of a group of boys."

"Where?"

"There on the extreme right."

"Good heavens—it will take a week to get the mud off! What's he been doing?"

"Mixing clay for the bricks. He'll need a good scrubbing, all right."

"Dad, did you buy my book?" Pasquelo called as he drew near.

"No, the bookstores I tried had never heard of it. Where did you get yours, Frank?"

"John loaned it to me. Ask him where to buy one."

"What do you think of the book, Frank?"

"I...don't have an opinion right now. I haven't spent much time with it. It's like the Bible in its moral teaching. The historical part of it is interesting. I would have more regard for it if there wasn't this wild tale about its origin...all this bosh about an angel appearing to a man who thought he had prophetic powers and telling him about the book being buried in a hill. If I believed in modern-day prophets I'd also accept witch doctors and ghosts."

"I raised the same question when talking with John. He replied with a quotation from the Bible: 'Surely the Lord God will do nothing, but he revealeth his secrets to his servants the prophets.' John said you had to accept

115

the fact of present-day revelation or admit that God wasn't at work anymore."

Margarita interrupted the discussion. "Come in," she invited. "Julia has just taken some cookies out of the oven, and the coffee is poured. Boys," she spoke to her future charges who stood nearby, "I know you're tired and hungry after kneading clay all afternoon, so wash up so you can have some cookies and milk."

"Are these the chaps you plan to house here?" Grant asked.

"Some of them are. Others belong to the village and have been helping out."

Grant preceded Frank into the kitchen and looked around for a place to put his hat. "This is the first time I've been in this part of your house, Señora Marquez. I didn't know you had a regular kitchen. I thought that bamboo shelter was the only place you had to prepare your meals."

"We brought the wood range with us from Laredo. I soon realized how practical an outdoor kitchen was, so my husband had mine built. I do most of my cooking out there."

"That seems inconvenient," Grant said.

"Not really. There are many advantages. For one, you don't heat the main part of the house in hot weather, and the smell of cooking doesn't permeate everything—including your clothes. And a small fire in the hearth doesn't use as much wood as the stove does."

"In rainy weather?"

"Then I cook in here. I'll be glad when our new kitchen is built."

"You have an ambitious program. Have you thought that you might be entitled to some federal aid?"

"We don't want it," Frank hastened to say. "At least not until we're convinced that we must have outside help. There are too many strings attached to public charity, and my greatest criticism of it is that by the time the administrators of the fund are paid there's nothing left for the needy. We don't want any interference. There's no reason why we can't care for our own poor and solve our own problems."

"Good for you, Frank. You should be in politics. Too many people depend on the federal government to work miracles for them without their making any effort to help themselves. Señora Marquez, I enjoyed the coffee and cookies." Grant arose and looked around. "Now where is my boy? I thought he was here."

"He's watching the men lay brick, no doubt," Frank told him.

"Let's go," Grant called through the window, and Pasquelo came running in. He picked up his weekend bag and followed Grant.

"I'll see you next Friday, Mamá," he called from the car.

Chapter 13

Frank came in exhausted. He had been aroused early that morning by the clangor of church bells. "Some saint being honored," he mused, "but must they start before daybreak?" He tried to go back to sleep but the persistent din prevented his doing so, and by the time the last echo died away the village donkeys had been inspired to praise...or was it lament? Then the dogs took up the strain. He crushed a pillow over his head in an effort to shut out the noise, but when the plop-plop of sandaled feet was added to the aggregate he gave up and arose. The swish-swish of Lola's broom told him she was sweeping the patio and the rhythm employed let him know she wanted to prepare his breakfast and get about more interesting tasks. He looked through the window into his garden. It was barely light, and the semigloom of early morning dimmed the whiteness of his lilies. By the time he was dressed Lola had his breakfast ready.

"Why are you up so early?" he asked.

"It isn't early for people who go to bed at a decent hour," she replied.

"I could have had another hour's sleep," he persisted. "I'm terribly tired."

"You should not have worked on the building yesterday, Mamá said." Frank noticed that whenever

118

Lola made a remark bordering on impertinence she usually attributed it to Margarita.

"The shelter has to be finished before the rains, and if we don't all pitch in and help the kids will still be sleeping in doorways this time next year."

"It's almost finished now. Pablo, Ernesto, and Ricardo will be out of jail today, Joe told me. They should be sober by now."

"They won't feel like working if they are."

"They will work," she said grimly. "The *jefe* will be here. They'll do the kitchen roof today or tomorrow, and Saturday we'll have a fiesta to celebrate. Already the girls are making paper flowers. The house will be decorated all over, the streetlights will burn until midnight, and we'll have fireworks."

"We can't have fireworks exploding near the old kitchen, Lola. That thatch could go up in flames in a second and we'd lose all we have stored there."

"The fireworks will be on the plaza." Lola spoke as if she were explaining a problem to a not-too-bright child. "Now if you'll go outside I'll clean the house. I have a lot to do today."

"Do you realize, Lola, that between you, Margarita, and Henrietta I'm ordered around and badgered as if I were married to all three of you?"

Lola giggled. "You need a little bossing," she told him.

Excitement permeated the entire village. School was dismissed on Thursday until the following Monday so that the students could help prepare for the big event. Crepe paper streamers were looped across the streets and lanes. The shelter was bright with the paper flowers Lola had spoken of. Food vendors had set up their booths and, early as it was, patrons were stopping by for coffee and tortillas or tamales lifted steaming hot from a large kettle. Even people from nearby pueblos were arriving by bus.

Lola had been up since before sunrise and had the Marquez home and Frank's place sparkling. When Grant and Pasquelo arrived she was trying to get the boys ready for the inspection she felt sure they would have to face. Anselmo would have no part of it. He had had a nourishing breakfast and was now ready to make a day of it on the town. He had never had a bath that he could remember and he didn't intend to break his record. He taunted the other boys and made a general nuisance of himself until Joe walked in. At sight of the young officer he darted across the yard and up the road. Lola lined her charges up and looked them over critically.

"You're a good-looking bunch of kids,' she told them, "and remember to take care of your clothes. Mamá worked hard to get them ready for the fiesta. People are going to watch you today, so behave yourselves."

Grant surveyed the shelter judicially. It was composed of one long room with a smaller annex for the kitchen. A fireplace occupied one end of the dormitory part of the building, and the hammocks

120

were drawn up out of the way. A dining table folded against the wall when not in use.

"It's very nice, Señora Marquez. I hope the villagers approve of it."

"Oh, they do! They've been looking forward to this day. It must be nearly time for the ceremony.... I see Henry coming. He's to start it; then Father Fidel will dedicate the shelter. You will excuse me, please. I must get the boys. I want them to be present."

"Here they come now with Frank and Pasquelo."

Margarita looked in the direction he indicated. "Anselmo isn't with them," she said. "He's going to be my biggest problem."

Henry's talk was brief, and he contrived to have Frank finish it. The teacher frowned but arose to complete Henry's speech. He congratulated the villagers on making El Abrigo possible and urged their continued support. Margarita was introduced as housemother, and the boys were officially welcomed.

"We have accepted you as our charges," he told them, "to see to your welfare—that you are fed, clothed, and comfortably housed. You must accept us as your teachers and guides. I expect to see every one of you in school Monday morning." Then Father Fidel took over, passing through the building with his swinging censer as he intoned his dedicatory prayer.

After further inspection of El Abrigo and a period of visiting, the people moved on to the plaza and the market. There was a brisk business around the open fires with the savory steam rising from pots of food.

By midnight most of the excitement had died down.

Margarita had worked in the hotel dining room all day and after its closing sat down for a moment before beginning her search for the boys. Lola and Frank found her there.

"Ready to call it a day?" Frank asked.

"As soon as I find Anselmo. There's Pasquelo. . .perhaps he's seen him."

"No, I haven't," the boy said, "but I'll look."

"Perhaps he's gone down to the shelter," Grant suggested.

Pasquelo returned to report that Anselmo was not in the building.

"Don't worry about him for the present, Margarita," Frank adivsed. "I'll look for him in the morning."

Margarita, Frank, Grant, and Pasquelo said their good-nights and soon were in their respective beds, sleeping soundly.

It seemed to Margarita that she had hardly closed her eyes when it was time to start another day. And morning brought a miniature revolution. Not one of the boys was ready to get up, and not one saw the need for washing face and hands. Sitting down at the table to eat was another new experience, and Frank had to be drafted into sitting at the head of the table to prevent chaos.

Anselmo finally presented himself for the meal, pausing diffidently at the door before entering. When he found that he was welcome, he swaggered in and took his place as though he was a paying guest.

Tooth brushing was another mountain. "Let their

teeth fall out, Mamá; they don't deserve to be helped!" Lola said.

"No, we're going to start out right," Margarita insisted, and she stood her ground until every toothbrush had been used, cleaned, and put away.

It was too early for church, so Lola decided to give the boys some religious instruction at home. Again Anselmo rebelled and disappeared the minute she left the room to get her prayer book. Upon her return Lola lined the rest of them up facing her. They learned to cross themselves, but after repeating 'Hail, Mary, full of grace,' a number of times they refused to greet the Virgin again. One youngster was even heard to commit her to a place where the fire is always well stoked. That concluded their theological training as far as Lola was concerned.

"You're nothing but a bunch of barbarians!" she told them as Margarita walked in.

"Perhaps it's a little early for religion, Lola. I think a better idea is to start them off with some practical responsibility—like cleaning the dormitory, folding their pajamas, and drawing their hammocks up out of the way."

The women were relieved when Frank took the boys over to the schoolhouse to introduce them to what he hoped would be their future daytime home.

Had Frank not taken charge of the boys Margarita couldn't have endured the weekend. Accustomed to the quiet routine of her home, she found the addition of this group of active youngsters like the descent of an avalanche on a peaceful Alpine village. The new life-style necessitated adjustments for the boys too—no begging, no bothering tourists, no slipping into a shop to grab an article that could be exchanged for food. They were well fed three times a day now, of course, but they were accustomed to taking what they wanted when they wanted it, and they found old habits hard to break. Knowing that the villagers kept a critical eye on her charges, Margarita was ever on guard, determined that there should be no reason for disapproval. Some of the townspeople, however, were lenient and often treated them to some trifle from the market. Frank saw Oscar Tamaya give them a ride on the manually operated merry-go-round. The boys conducted themselves well until Anselmo joined them, which he did every time he saw them receiving some special attention. He was on the spot when the ride was offered and climbed onto a horse with great bravado and began slapping the pony and yelling, then looking around to see if he was being admired. When Arturo Dominguez bought them *frescos*, in his effort to be the first to receive one Anselmo knocked the filled container out of the merchant's hands. The boys laughed heartily while Anselmo strutted around, a pleased grin on his face.

"What a bad apple!" Frank muttered as he drew near to reprimand the boy. But Anselmo darted off without his ice when he saw the teacher approaching.

"I'm afraid you're going to have trouble with that one," Arturo said.

"I'm sure we will," Frank agreed.

"It might be wise to get rid of him before he ruins the others."

"It may be necessary to separate them, but I hate to start out with an admission of failure."

That evening Frank discussed with Margarita the advisability of barring Anselmo from the shelter.

"No, we can't do that. . . not yet, anyway. We must give him—and ourselves—a chance. This is a new experience for us as well as for him. We must have patience."

But her patience wore thin during the following weeks. Anselmo defied nearly all rules and regulations at El Abrigo. He never came near the place except to eat and sleep. The other boys accepted their tasks, and some even took pride in doing them well. Frank got Anselmo into the classroom by taking him each morning, but during unguarded moments he would dash out and run to the plaza if there was a crowd where he might lose himself. . . or to the hills if he felt detection was too likely in the village.

Included in the duties divided among the boys was taking care of the horse. Since the one assigned to this was permitted to ride the animal to and from the watering trough it was, by far, the most popular task. On the morning it was Pablo's assignment he got up immediately and went out to the pen. A few minutes later he came running back shouting, "Señora, señora, the horse is gone!"

Margarita came to the door. "Bolivar gone?" She looked out to the empty lot. "Was the gate open?"

125

"No, señora, the gate's locked."

Lola had been getting Frank's breakfast, but when she heard the commotion she hurried outside to learn the cause.

"He didn't fly over the fence!" she said sarcastically and marched into the dormitory to count bodies. Two were missing.

"It's Anselmo," she said on her return.

"Every boy loves a horse," Margarita said. "I suppose the temptation was too great. What will we ever do with him?"

"Kill him," was Lola's immediate suggestion. "Save the government the cost of hanging him."

"He is hard to manage," Margarita admitted. "Let's get breakfast over, then we'll look for Bolivar."

When he learned of Anselmo's latest escapade, Frank said, "I'll walk up to the village and see if anyone saw him leave."

"And I'll go to the highway. Bonificio goes to work early and may have seen him pass the garage," Lola said.

But neither had to go far, for when they reached the road they saw Joe approaching on foot with Anselmo in tow, leading the horse.

"This is the limit!" the officer declared when he got within hearing distance. "He starts out stealing peanuts, now a horse. Next time he'll be robbing a bank. In spite of Señora Marquez' theory about ruling with love, this demands punishment. He has broken the law."

"I agree with you, Joe. There is such a thing as

carrying forbearance too far," Frank agreed.

Margarita waited by the well.

"He will have to be punished, Señora Marquez," Joe said. "I've sent word to Remundo to meet us here."

"He's only a child, Joe. The horse is home again, and no harm has been done."

"Except to his own character and the possible effect his thievery could have on the other boys," Joe said. "We've had trouble with him since the day he came to the valley. He's a born criminal."

"I don't think children are born bad. Circumstances and environment make them what they are. Anselmo had a bad start. I think you should overlook this...and I'll try harder to understand him."

Not wanting to pursue the argument Joe said, "Here comes Remundo. He'll decide what must be done."

Margarita repeated her stand to the police chief as soon as he appeared. "He's just a child," she kept saying.

Remundo finally gave in. "All right, Señora Marquez. Although I think I'm making a mistake, we'll drop the matter. I feel that he should be locked up until he learns what a good thing he has here at El Abrigo. We'll give him another chance after Joe administers a good spanking. This act cannot go unpunished. Joe, you take it from here...and give him something he'll remember. It may save him from greater punishment in the future."

"All right, a good licking it is—like my dad used to give me. Here, Pablo, you take the horse. Frank, is your house available?"

"Of course."

Margarita went inside and tried to close her ears to the cries of pain she expected to hear—but they never came. When Joe returned, replacing his belt, the culprit preceded him as defiant as ever. He was trembling, whether from anger or physical suffering Margarita couldn't tell, but suddenly she was filled with compassion and went to him with extended arms. When she reached him, he turned and spit in her face. She automatically drew back her hand and slapped him. He cursed her, grabbed her hands, and continued to spit. Her cries attracted Frank and Joe, and they came running. This time Joe didn't ask for seclusion to mete out punishment, and Margarita didn't interfere. A more subdued boy stood before Joe when he again replaced his belt.

"Come over here, Anselmo. I want to have a man-to-man talk with you," he said. "I didn't enjoy this episode any more than you did, but you forced it on me. And don't think for a minute that I won't repeat it if I have to. I'm fed up with you and your nonsense, and I'm laying down the law. Hereafter you'll be in school when it starts and stay until you're dismissed. You'll accept your share of the work here, and when you're given a job you'll do it well. If we have any more trouble with you I'll take you to Cuernavaca and put you in a place where you cannot escape. You'll eat only what you can beg from people passing by the jail. Choose now what you want to do. You can stay on here, or you can go with me to Cuernavaca. Which will it be?"

"I'll stay."

"Good, you're a smart boy. Now wash up for breakfast," Joe waited while he drew water from the well and washed his face and hands. Lola came out with a clean towel, and Joe, with an arm around the boy's shoulders, ushered him into the dining room.

"Señora Marquez, can you spare a hungry man a cup of coffee and a roll?" Joe asked.

"I'll do better than that, Joe. I've prepared breakfast for you and the Professor in my kitchen. Señor Bera brought us a case of eggs last week, and I've scrambled some. Lola is waiting to serve you."

Chapter 14

"Well, Frank, it's time you showed up. I've been looking for you every Friday since we moved in."

"I'm pretty busy in the valley since we've opened the home, John. Say...you certainly have a lovely place. Evidently teaching pays more here than it does in Alhaja."

"We're pleased with it. It was terribly run down and priced reasonably low or we couldn't have afforded it. We've made a lot of repairs, but as you see we still have plenty of work ahead of us. Isobel is more content than I've ever seen her. She's spent a lot of time hopping from one place to another ever since she left college. Do you remember my sister?"

"Wasn't she the little roughneck that had all the boys afraid of her?"

"That's Isobel! She's tamed down a lot since then...and now the boys chase her. Come on out to the patio. That's where she's usually at work planting, pruning, or trying to revive shrubs that have been neglected." John opened the door and invited Frank into the *sala*.

The floor, Frank noticed, was of red brick, polished to a satin finish. A fireplace filled one end of the room, its mantle banked with sprays of scarlet bougainvillaea. One wall supported shelves filled with books.

Completing the furnishings were a large sofa, a coffee table, and an assortment of chairs with small tables conveniently near.

"It's sparsely furnished, but Isobel hopes to replace all this with some really good pieces eventually. We do have electricity and indoor plumbing," he explained with a smile.

"I don't notice any scarcity. You've seen my place—now that's a model of barest necessities."

"Well...come on, we'll try to locate Sis." John led the way through the house, calling her as he went.

"I'm here, Johnny," she spoke from the top of a ladder.

"Why are you risking your life on that contraption?" he demanded.

"You might steady it and help me down instead of yelling at me," she scolded.

He obeyed and gave her a gentle shake as soon as she was safely on the patio floor. "Remember Frank? You were pretty small when we ran around together."

"I've heard about him all my life. How are you, Frank?"

He looked at her with interest as he took the hand she extended. Her shoulder-length hair glistened in the sun, and he noted her smile was...well...provocative. He anticipated a better acquaintance.

"Let's sit over here where we can talk in comfort," John suggested. "Tell us about your project, Frank. It's a wonderful thing you're doing, but whatever gave you the idea?"

"I really don't know, unless it was seeing how

Margarita took in three strays and gave them her care and her love. When I look back, I don't believe I thought of those children as human before. They were so dirty and their hair so matted they looked more like animals."

"Do you think your rehabilitation program will work?"

"Right now things are running smoothly, but I never know for how long. We had a lot of adjustments to make, and we still hit snags frequently."

"It's a pity more communities don't follow your example. Perhaps some day they will," John said.

"I hope so, and I also hope that they will learn from us to avoid some of the mistakes we make."

"The chances for error in such a venture are sure to be endless. You know, I envy you, Frank. It seems to me that you're on the ground floor of something really big."

"I hope so. We're going to work at it."

"I wonder why someone hasn't instituted a similar program here. Goodness knows we have the need. The plazas swarm with children who, to all appearances, have no home and certainly no supervision."

"Our small village gives us an advantage, I think. We have fewer people to consider and more time to consider them and their problems."

"You don't have the distractions that we have here," Isobel said. "There are so many demands for our time and attention—school activities, movies, ball games...."

"We seldom have movies in Alhaja—and never

132

lectures or bridge games," Frank admitted. "These I can do without, but I do miss ball games. I drive into Cuernavaca occasionally when I know an interesting one is scheduled."

"How would you like to see a game tonight? Our school is playing, and Pasquelo is on the team."

"Great!"

"Okay. We'll have an early supper. I'll call Grant and tell him we'll pick up him and Pasquelo on our way." When he called Grant excused himself, since Pasquelo had to be at school early, but he promised to meet them at the entrance to the field.

Isobel brought a wave of perfume into the room as she joined the men.

"Isn't that scent a little heady for a ball game?" John asked.

"I'm not going with you," she informed her brother.

"Casco?" John asked.

"*Dr.* Casco," she corrected him.

"Again? I hope you aren't planning to marry him. Why don't you come with us?"

"No, thanks, I'll stick with Atticus."

"Suit yourself, but you're making a big mistake. Come on, Frank, let's leave her to her fate. I tell you, there's no accounting for women's tastes!"

"Do you think she's serious about him?" Frank asked as they left the house.

"I don't know. He's very attentive. I think this is the fourth time this week that she's been out with him."

"What's your objection to him, John? Seems to me

133

that a medical man would be an acceptable husband, all other things being equal."

"I don't think they are. I really can't put my finger on my reason for feeling as I do. I can accept a man smelling of shaving soap or lotion, but for one to enter a room exuding the fragrance of gardenias—that's too much. Then, when he pulls his carefully folded handkerchief from his pocket and almost asphyxiates you with his perfume, I am actually embarrassed for him. My car's in the garage—over this way."

"Why not take mine? It's already out."

"Space will likely be at a premium, Frank, and mine will take up less room." John unlocked the door, backed his car out, and Frank got in beside him.

"Isobel is certainly beautiful."

"I agree, but she's surely a responsibility. Let's talk of something else."

"All right. What chance does your team have of winning tonight's game?"

"Both teams are good. It should be an exciting contest."

Grant was waiting as he had promised, and they joined the crowd pressing through the gates.

"Looks as if you're going to have a good attendance," Frank said.

"Yes, our games are usually well supported. This is Pasquelo's first big one, isn't it, Grant?"

"Yes, and he's going to be hard to live with if his side loses." They found seats and settled down to enjoy the game.

It was evident from the first that it would be a close

one, but the visiting team started edging ahead, and Pasquelo's lost by a point. He was crushed when he met the men after the game.

"This isn't the only chance you'll get to play, son," Grant tried to console him. "There'll be other games, and you'll improve with each one."

"But I shouldn't have missed that ball!" he reprimanded himself.

"Listen, Pasquelo, no one error lost the game. I'm sorry you slipped up, but yours wasn't the only mistake made."

"I need a lot more practice," he declared.

"Pasquelo, did the village ever have a ball team?" Frank asked.

"No, there never was anyone there with the time or the knowledge to organize one. We used to kick a ball around, but we didn't know the rules."

"When you come home next weekend why don't you form a team? I never played but I know enough from watching to umpire the game. That may be the key to one of our problems."

"I'd like to try it."

"Good! I'll buy the equipment, and we'll be all set when you arrive."

Pasquelo's enthusiasm for a hometown ball team mounted all during the week. Frank had left money with him to buy what was needed, and when Grant picked him up each day after school they went immediately to the sporting goods store. He even lingered over the rack of uniforms.

"You don't need those until you have your team organized," Grant told him. "You have a long way to go before you're ready for them. By that time, if you're good enough, perhaps one of the businessmen will sponsor you and furnish the uniforms."

"I never thought of that," he said, obviously pleased.

Saturday finally came, and Pasquelo lost no time in doing his chores.

"I have to deliver eggs to the hotel this morning, Pasquelo; we'll run down to the valley from there. Get your things together and load them in the car." Grant followed Pasquelo outside, then paused to add, "Let's take your mother another case of eggs. We haven't taken any for several weeks. Put your things in the trunk. We'd better keep the eggs where we can steady them when we go over the rough spots."

Grant went back to the house and when he returned Manuela trailed after him carrying a large package.

"What's that?" Pasquelo asked.

"Some chickens. Thought your mother could use them, and we're overstocked. Do you have everything you need?"

"Yes, sir."

"All right, let's go."

"Where are you going, Lola?" Margarita asked early Saturday morning.

"To church to pray," the girl answered.

"I thought you reserved your supplications for Sunday."

"We can't wait until tomorrow. Do you know that we don't have enough food in the house to feed the boys tonight?"

"I know. We've often scraped the bottom of the barrel toward the end of the month, but this time we'll have to move the barrel and scrape under it. If the boys didn't have such big appetites! There's no such thing as a leftover at El Abrigo."

"Have you told the professor about it?"

"No, he has his own problems. This one is ours. We'll manage some way, and let's keep this to ourselves, Lola. If the villagers knew they would think I wasn't doing a very good job."

"Well, I'm going to pray now. I won't be gone long."

Margarita decided to check the kitchen again, hoping the girls might have overlooked a basket of beans. But she found that Julia had preceded her on the same errand. "What will we do about supper?" she asked quietly.

"Is there no corn meal left?"

"Not nearly enough. Did Señor Orosco send his usual amount of masa?"

"Yes, everyone has kept his part of the bargain, both in food and money. Some have done more. We're simply feeding more than we planned. We thought ten was a safe number to ask provisions for, but now we have fourteen regulars and usually several extras at every meal."

"It seems to me that the extras have become regulars," Julia reflected.

"But we can't turn a child away, even though we know his parents could and should provide for him."

"You can't ask Señora Hernandez for help?"

"No, indeed. She has already done far more than her share. She always does. But I wish something could be done to get the parents to help feed their children," Margarita sighed. "I suppose I'll have to tell Señor Faz after all. I can't let the boys go hungry, and it's another week before our supplies come in. But I hate to do it—it's like admitting failure." The arrival of the Bera car interrupted her train of thought. Pasquelo bounded up the steps and submitted to her embrace.

"How've you been, Mamá, and where are the boys?" he asked.

"I'm fine, and the boys are working over at the school."

"On Saturday?"

"They're painting the building."

"Where shall I put this, Señora Marquez?" Grant stepped onto the porch.

"What is it, Señor Bera?"

"Another case of eggs."

Margarita stood with open mouth. "A case of eggs?"

"Yes, my hens are better at production than I am at sales. They're piling up on me."

Margarita covered her face to hide her tears.

Grant stood by awkwardly. He finally managed to say, "I never knew that you felt this way about my bringing eggs when I had an oversupply. I don't mean

138

to offend you. I just hoped you could use them. If the boys' appetites are any match for Pasquelo's, a case of eggs won't last long."

"I'm not offended; I'm just very, very grateful. I've been on the edge of hysteria watching our dwindling food supply."

"Are your sponsors not supporting you?"

"Oh, yes—not a one has failed. We got along fine until some of the villagers, who contribute nothing, began sending their children down here for meals—all of them. I simply cannot stretch the food provided for ten to feed twice that number."

"Does Frank know?"

"Know what?" Frank had knocked, but when he received no answer had let himself in.

"That this lady has been having to feed half of Alhaja and has run out of food," Grant explained.

"And Mamá has spent all her own money from sewing to buy beans and meal and rice." Lola had walked in in time to add her bit.

"How in the world . . ."

"I'll tell you how in the world. It's all those extra kids we have to feed. The Ruiz send theirs, the Rivas send three of theirs . . ."

"Lola, that will do. We'll work this out some way," Margarita said, but Frank contradicted her.

"No, you won't work it out! I got you into this, and I'll handle it. Who else is shoving children off on you?"

"When all those children come in and struggle for places at the table I simply cannot turn them away. Señor Bera brought us a case of eggs. . . ."

"Eggs!" Lola shouted. "The sweet little Virgin answered my prayer!"

"In just a few days we'll be getting our money and supplies. Perhaps something will turn up in the meantime," Margarita continued over Lola's triumphant outburst.

"It's going to turn up right now! I had no idea this was going on. I saw the children here at times, but I supposed they came to play," Frank said. "I'll see Joe and have him talk with the parents. We'll put a stop to this little racket." He turned to leave and bumped into Grant who had gone to the car for the chickens.

"I'm killing off my old hens, and my freezer is full. I brought along a dozen ready for cooking. . . . Now don't start crying again. I can't take it. Come on. Let's go to the village and buy what you need to tide you over. Don't argue, just come along and tell me what to buy."

"I don't like to do this, Señor Bera. It isn't your responsibility, and you've done more than enough already."

"We're wasting time, Margarita. Let's go."

Lola waited until they left, then turned to the altar where the Virgin occupied the center of the shrine. "Holy Mother," she said sternly, "I've been thinking this over, and I'm irritated! You had nothing to do with Señora Bera's bringing those eggs! He had left Mexico City before I even thought of going to the church. Why did you let me spend my last peso for a candle to burn before you? I don't like this one bit. You cheated me!"

140

Chapter 15

John paused at Isobel's open door to watch as she completed applying her makeup. She smiled at his reflection in the mirror.

"Will I do?" she asked.

"What's up?" he parried. "I thought that yellow rigging was reserved for special occasions."

"This is one of them. I'm going to dinner and the ballet with Frank."

"Hmmm.... From the frequency of his visits I'd judge that he's running neck and neck with the doctor."

"No, Frank is at least two laps ahead of Atticus."

"Good. I suppose this means I'll have to eat supper alone again tonight."

"Now, Johnny, don't make me feel guilty. You talk as though you're being neglected. I've spoiled you—that's the whole trouble."

"I thought it was the other way around."

"I seldom leave you alone except on weekends. Why don't you date? I know at least a half dozen girls who'd like to go out with you. Why not ask one of them?"

"Can't afford it. Remember, I'm buying a house. Besides, I'm too busy, which reminds me that I have Sunday's sermon to finish."

"Make it a good one. I'm taking Frank to church this week."

"Does he know that?"

"Yes, that was the condition for tonight's date."

"Why?"

She hesitated for a moment, then said, "Johnny, I have a confession to make. I'm beginning to think a lot of Frank—too much, perhaps."

"He's one of the best, Bel."

"I know, but I can't afford to become too involved as long as he's indifferent to the church. I've been thinking that if he becomes better acquainted with what we believe he'll be more interested."

"Frank has had plenty of exposure, Bel. I've been trying for years to get him involved, but he's as apathetic as ever. I was disappointed that our tour didn't arouse an interest in Mexico's ancient history. I felt that a study of that might lead to his investigating the Book of Mormon. He still sees no connection between the two."

"I know, and that worries me."

"Well, be careful. I don't want to see you get hurt."

"I'm going to avoid that if I can. There go the chimes. Will you let Frank in while I make a final survey?"

"Sure," John opened the gate to admit his friend. "Come in, come in, Frank," he invited. "Have a seat. How are things in the valley?"

Frank took the chair indicated. "Things don't change much in Alhaja except that we seem to be getting a few more tourists than usual. . .which helps the economy."

"And the shelter?"

"Getting along okay, I think. I've been so busy at school that I really haven't spent much time with the boys, outside of the classroom that is. Since they're learning to study they get into less mischief and don't bother Margarita as much. At least I haven't been called on to discipline any of them recently. I'm sure the ball team has something to do with their reform, too."

"How's it doing?"

"Remarkably well. It was pretty hard to teach them teamwork, but Pasquelo kept after them until they shaped up. And there are some good little athletes."

"You still have to oversee them, I suppose."

"They're on their own much of the time. You've probably noticed that I spend most of my weekends in the city."

"I do see you around occasionally," John replied. "By the way, I picked up an El Paso paper while I was at Grant's one day and saw an article you'd written. Not bad!"

"Thanks. I've also done a few things for a travel magazine. I'm glad I went on that tour. . .it gives me grist for my mill!"

"Could that be responsible for the increased traffic in the valley?"

"I doubt that it's had time yet, but I'm hoping."

"I've never known two men who had so much to talk about!" Isobel stood in the doorway.

"Did you expect us to sit here in silence while you changed your face?" John kidded.

"You're worth waiting for," Frank assured her. "Are we ready to go?"

"We'd better, if we expect to see all of the ballet."

"Is your brother here?" Pasquelo called through the open door to Isobel.

"No, he had a teachers' meeting after school and isn't home yet. Can I help you?"

"I don't think so. He wanted me to do something at church Sunday morning, and I came to see what it was."

"You'll have to wait for him, Pasquelo. Come on back and visit with me until he gets here. Hand me that book out of the chair so you can sit down. When Frank was here last night we began reminiscing about our college days. I got my Graceland yearbook out to show him some pictures, and I didn't put it away afterwards."

"Where is Graceland? May I look at the book?"

"Of course. Graceland is in the United States, in the state of Iowa."

Pasquelo took the book and turned the pages slowly. "Why did you choose a college so far away instead of going to our own university?"

"I went to a university in Saltillo after I got out of Graceland. It was Johnny's idea. During my teen years I began running with a pretty wild bunch. Since my

144

parents were dead Johnny was trying to be mother and father to me, and I think he was afraid. Although I had been baptized into the church, I was not really converted. He felt that if I went to our church college my faith would be strengthened."

"Was it?"

"Indeed it was! I boarded in the home of one of our elders. I think he could have made a Christian of Robert Ingersoll."

Pasquelo continued to turn the pages of the book, then paused to ask, "Is this snow?"

"It certainly is. Let me get my photo album—I have some beautiful snow scenes in that." She went to her room and came back with the book. "Now let me show you some views of the campus in winter. Here, take the album and start at the first. It's really a pictorial diary. I began taking pictures the week I arrived and sent them on to Johnny so he would know what I was doing."

"You're a good photographer. But you didn't take all of these—here's one of you in a baseball cap."

"I did it on a dare. There was this one boy I didn't like. . . . He called me 'hot tamale,' and I wanted to get back at him. He was on the baseball team, and one day when he was batting he missed a ball that a two-year-old child could have hit. . . at least that's what I told him. He dared me to do better. In fact, he bet me a dinner and show against my doing his laundry for a month if I could use a bat any better than he did. Since I had played baseball with the boys of the neighborhood when I was younger I took him up on it.

There was to be a practice game the next day and it was agreed that I would, as Gary put it, 'make a fool of myself before a crowd.' My friends sympathized with me, and some even offered to help me with the laundry. Well, I hit a home run on the first try. The team said it was pure luck and challenged me to try again. So I hit the ball a second time. After my third success Gary admitted defeat and offered to pay his debt."

"What did he say about your batting average?"

"He claimed I took unfair advantage. He said no boy could keep his mind on the game while playing opposite a girl in shorts."

"I know Mamá will want me to get my education in Mexico, but I'd certainly like to see other parts of the world. Until I went on that tour, I had never been farther from home than Mexico City."

"It would be nice if you could see some of the States. About all I saw of it outside of Iowa was from the bus—but it was fascinating. Here comes Johnny. If you'll excuse me I'll see what Delia has planned for supper."

Chapter 16

"Seguro, why do accidents always happen to you?" Didn't you see Rosie's bucket of water here on the patio? And if you had to trip over it, couldn't you have stumbled into it while it was clean instead of waiting until after she'd used it to scrub the floor?" Lola sent her barrage of questions down at the small boy.

"The water fell out," he said looking at the small lake spreading over the clean tiles.

"Yes, the water fell out when you fell in."

"What happened, Lola? Rosie's in there threatening to grind someone's bones to powder. Who's the victim this time? Oh, Seguro! I might have known," Margarita said, tousling his hair. She started to the garden but paused when she saw Frank crossing the yard toward her.

"Someone have an accident?" he asked, eyeing the patio.

"Nothing serious," Margarita replied. "What have you there?"

"I just received this letter from John. He and Isobel are going to drive over to the lake for the weekend and want us to go with them. There's no reason why you can't get away, is there?"

"Of course not," Lola took over before Margarita had time to answer. "It will be good for her to get away. I can take care of things, but if I should need help I can call Joe."

"I don't know, Frank. Sometimes the boys get unruly when both of us are away...."

"Lola can handle them. I often think that she would make a very efficient policewoman. She and Joe would make a fine pair."

Lola ignored this teasing about the young officer's attention. "Of course I can take care of them. I'll look after them as though I had borne them myself... which I did not, praise God!"

"I'll have to take the two youngest with me," Margarita warned.

"No problem.... I'll write John that we'll be there."

Not only Isobel and John but Grant and Pasquelo waited for Frank's car. Pasquelo took charge of his mother at once.

"You're to ride with us," he directed. "You sit in front with Dad and I'll ride back here with the children. He says we're to relieve you of their care."

"That will be nice," she replied, and obediently transferred to Grant's car.

"Leave your car here, John. You can ride with Isobel and me."

"Why not go in mine? I got it serviced for the trip."

"There's more room for our trappings in the wagon. I'll help you change over." The shift was soon made, and they started out. As soon as they reached the vacation spot Frank's tent was put up for the women before the rest of the equipment was unloaded.

"You can put on your swimsuits and enjoy the water while we set up camp," John told them. Isobel made no objection, but Margarita took her small boys in tow as Pasquelo's sense of responsibility vanished at sight of the lake. He was in the water within minutes after the car stopped.

"Margarita, I'll take charge of the little ones. Go ahead—enjoy the lake," Grant told her.

"I don't know how to swim, and I don't possess a suit," she replied.

"Well, at least you can wade in the shallow water," he insisted. She took off her shoes and hose and ventured in.

They established a routine the first morning. While Margarita and Isobel prepared breakfast the men fished for the noon and evening meals, which they took turns cooking. John and Grant shared the care of the little boys during the day, leaving Margarita free to walk along the lakeside enjoying a freedom she seldom experienced. Pasquelo emerged from the water only to eat and sleep. Isobel and Frank were together constantly, swimming, strolling along the shore, and quietly conversing.

It was the last evening of their holiday, and the fire had become softly glowing coals. Margarita had put her charges to bed in the tent. Pasquelo, still in swim trunks, made periodic dashes into the water.

"Shall we take a final walk?" Frank took Isobel's hands and drew her to her feet.

"Anyone want to come with us?" she asked.

"Not me," John said. "I've used muscles the past two days I haven't exercised in months. . . . I don't want to antagonize them anymore." Margarita and Grant also refused.

The couple strolled off, and for a time walked casually side by side. Then Frank drew Isobel's arm through the crook in his and they fell into step. They discussed various subjects, from personal and professional problems to world affairs.

"I think we'd better turn back," Isobel suggested. "I can't see the campfire anymore."

"They've probably let it die down. Let's sit here and talk."

"Isn't that what we've been doing?"

"Not on the subject I have in mind." He smoothed a place on the lake's edge for her and sat down beside her. There was a prolonged silence while Frank skipped stones over the surface of the water. Then he took her hand in his.

"Isobel, how does a man go about telling a woman that he loves her and wants her for his wife? Up until recently I have felt that I was not in a position where I could afford to marry. I think I am now financially able to support a wife. I'm ready for marriage and a home."

"Are you asking me to marry you?"

"Of course I am!"

Isobel was thoughtful for a moment. "Thank you, Frank, but no," she said.

"Why?"

150

"There are many reasons—mainly my faith and your lack of it."

"You're making union with your church a condition of our marriage?"

"No, although if I were marrying I'd prefer a man with my convictions."

"You're making a mountain out of a molehill."

"I don't think so. Perhaps I have fanciful ideas about marriage. To many people it's just a physical union. That isn't enough for me. If I every marry it will be a complete welding of mind and spirit as well as body. Perhaps I'm asking too much."

"You're asking the impossible. I don't want to lose my identity...no matter how much I love you." He released her hand, and she withdrew it to rest on her knee.

"I'd never ask that, and any man who would yield to that sort of situation wouldn't be worth marrying. If two people are in spiritual accord, I believe that everything else will fall into place. Perhaps I'm a dreamer...but that's the way I feel. You spoke a moment ago of being settled. You're far from it, Frank."

"Me?"

"Yes, you are spiritually and mentally unsettled."

"Over what?"

"The Book of Mormon. Right now you're in a sea of indecision. You've had proof of the divinity of the book in fulfillment of its prophecies in the Bible, in archaeological findings, and in ancient native records. You can't reject it entirely, yet you won't completely

151

accept it. I can't understand. . . . It all seems so simple to me."

"Is that all you have to say?"

"Yes."

"Final?"

"Final!"

"Shall we go?"

She arose, and with arms swinging free, they returned to camp.

Chapter 17

The day had been sultry and oppressive since its beginning. The boys had finished their Saturday chores and were free to do as they wished, but the temperature discouraged all activities—except bickering. Margarita had had to settle a dozen arguments, and her head ached from the strain. As she looked over to where Gallo and Seguro were playing, she regained her faith in boys. They could amuse themselves for hours without disagreement. She smiled as she watched the changing expressions on their small, brown faces.

Her pleasure suddenly turned to horror when, a few feet away, she saw a rattler slithering toward them. She dared not warn them, for any movement might startle it into striking. A strangled cry of alarm died in her throat, but Anselmo, coming across the patio with his slingshot, heard her muffled moan. His eyes followed to where her gaze was focused. Without a word he picked up a stone, took careful aim, and let it fly. It caught the snake just behind the head. The blow didn't kill it but did send it writhing off in the opposite direction. Before it had gone far, however, Anselmo grabbed a hoe and finished it off. There was a dull thud behind him, and when he looked around

Margarita was crumpled on the ground. He was beside her in a moment, cradling her in his arms.

"Mamá! Mamá!" he kept calling, then when she didn't respond he began shouting to the boys. They came running.

"Tell Lola Mamá has hurt herself. . . and hurry!"

The confusion aroused Margarita in time to hear Anselmo give his orders. Her heart skipped a beat. It was the first time he had ever called her Mamá, although the rest of the boys had acknowledged her in this way almost from the first. She burst into tears and held him close. By the time Lola arrived she was nearly hysterical, and Anselmo had to explain what had happened. He was quite the hero, but for once, admiration had no effect on him.

Margarita got to her feet, but she was still tembling. "Lola, get all the children inside, and examine the little boys to see if there are any scratches on them."

"The snake didn't bite 'em, Mamá," Anselmo assured her. "He didn't even coil."

"Better keep them inside anyway until we find the mate," Lola advised. "Snakes always travel in pairs. And Mamá, you'd better lie down. You don't look so good. Anselmo, if you'll draw some cold water from the well we'll bathe her face."

He ran to obey. Lola applied the first cold pack, and Anselmo observed closely. Then he took over.

The news spread rapidly through the village and the yard was soon filled with the curious, wanting to see the snake and hear firsthand how Anselmo had handled the matter. Frank rushed in as soon as he

154

heard of it and stood in open-mouthed wonder when he saw Anselmo's tender ministrations.

"I wish you could have been here to see how quick-witted Anselmo was. No man could have handled this affair better. Gallo and Seguro would certainly have been bitten but for him. I'll love him as long as I live."

Anselmo continued to hold the wet towel against Margarita's head until she said, "I'm all right now, Anselmo...and thank you for everything."

Lola appeared in the doorway and said, "Anselmo, Max Durango says you couldn't have hit a snake standing that distance from it. Come out here and show him how it's done." Anselmo obeyed and Lola followed him out to see that there was no heckling. She might scold the boys, yell at them for some broken rule, and threaten all sorts of dire punishments, but no one else was allowed that privilege.

"How did you tame the tiger?" Frank asked Margarita as the boys left the room. "I've never seen this side of him."

"Neither have I. I suppose it was having patience...and I sometimes think that he began changing his attitude right after the horse episode when Joe had to punish him. Perhaps he realized that we cared enough about his doing right to discipline him when it was necessary. There's been a great tragedy in his life, Frank."

A tragedy? What makes you think that?"

"Well, as you and Father Fidel advised, we've encouraged the boys to tell us anything they remember about their families and their life before they came here. Most of them have talked freely, and I think that has helped us understand them better and make allowances for some of the things they have done. But Anselmo has never mentioned any part of his life, and as you know he has adjusted slowly. One day when we were alone I asked him about his parents and if he had any brothers or sisters. His face turned white and he trembled all over. Without replying he ran from me. I'll always regret my probing questions for I know I opened an old wound. Since then Lola and I have worked very hard to include him in all our planning and have deferred to him in making decisions. Although he still remains aloof, I know he appreciates our attention, and today we crossed a wide gulf. . . . He called me Mamá."

Chapter 18

"Mamá, Father Fidel is here to see you."

"Who's done what now, Lola? Has someone skipped confession or gone to sleep during mass?" Margarita was measuring the dormitory windows for curtains.

"No, I think he wants to talk to you about me."

"You!" There was genuine alarm in Margarita's voice as she turned to face Lola.

"No, I haven't missed confession or mass. Joe's papá is with him, that's why I think he wants to talk to you about Joe and me getting married."

"Why didn't Joe come to me?"

"His father's old-fashioned and wants it done this way."

Margarita discarded her apron, smoothed her hair, and went in to welcome her guests.

"Señora Marquez, you will excuse our intrusion in the busy part of the day, please. Perhaps Lola explained the reason for it," the priest began.

"Not entirely," was Margarita's reply.

"This is most irregular," he added.

"What is, Father?"

Since the priest seemed to be making no progress Señor Morales took over. "Senora Marquez, ordinarily I would have approached you with Joe's godfather to ask your consent to my son and your daughter's

157

marriage. Because the man is somewhere in the United States and hasn't been heard from for fifteen years, I asked Father Fidel to act as his substitute." He paused for a moment, then continued, "I'm not at all pleased about this marriage, but Joe will have no one else. He's our only child, he has been to school in Cuernavaca..."

"Señor Morales thinks Joe could have done much better in the choice of a wife," Father Fidel explained.

"I doubt that!" Margarita said defensively. "Lola is a dear, sweet, virtuous girl. She is a good housekeeper, an excellent cook, and no one can deny that she is lovely."

"She may be all of that, Señora Marquez, but if you had not adopted her my son could not marry her."

"And why not?"

"We could never have accepted the daughter of that Juanita and who knows what man," Señor Morales said firmly.

"Well, I don't see how taking my name makes any difference. She's still Juanita's daughter," Margarita countered.

"It makes a big difference to me. Marquez is a good name."

Margarita ignored the compliment. "I'll discuss this with Lola," she said, rising.

"As soon as you have made your decision, will you let me know when to return?" the father asked.

"I'll get the message to you," she promised.

The men bowed out and Margarita went back to her work. Joe dropped by later for a cup of coffee.

158

"Joe, did you set the priest on me?" she asked.

"No, Señora Marquez, that was Papá's idea. I knew you wouldn't be pleased, but he was determined to go the old route and we can't afford to buck him. He's going to give us the house and land where he and Mamá lived when they were first married. I can't offend him. Besides, he's really a good guy. I'm sorry if it was a bother."

"It's just that I wasn't anticipating such a visit, and now I'm not sure what's expected of me. But I'll ask Henrietta; she'll know. Lola told me that you were willing for her to continue helping me here for a while. It will mean a lot to me, for she's my 'right hand.' "

"Well, I'm often out of the village on patrol and when I'm away, after she gets our own work done, it's all right for her to help you here. But she can't work anywhere else!"

"I appreciate that, Joe. I've know for some time that I would soon have to give her up. I haven't been blind to these visits you've made to check on the boys."

"It *was* a good excuse," he admitted.

"Chico, please bring me a basket. There are a lot of ripe tomatoes that must be picked at once." The boy ran to the storeroom and returned with the container.

"Your onions look terribly dry. Have you watered them today?" Margarita asked.

"No, Mamá, not yet. I've got this many big ones." He held up four fingers. "Can I take them to Dorina?"

"Yes, I'm sure she can use them. When you do that,

159

come and water the rest so they will continue growing." Margarita watched him for a moment then returned to her own work. She looked up later to see Lola leave the house and head for the garden.

"Mamá," she spoke in a loud whisper, "did Chico tell you?"

"About his onions? Yes, I told him to take them to Dorina."

"No, no,...it's the Moraleses! They're here to talk about Joe and me!"

"I'm sorry, Lola. Chico didn't tell me that. I'll go right in."

"What will Joe's parents think? They've been sitting in there for half an hour."

"You should have called me sooner. I'll explain my tardiness—I'm sure they'll understand." And Margarita hurried in with profuse apologies.

The guests were inclined at first to be a little restrained but Margarita won them with her graciousness, and they left as friends.

Joe came in soon after. "I see my folks have been here," he said, helping himself from a bowl of fruit.

"I like your parents, Joe," Margarita told him.

"So do I. They're the best...and I sure want them to like Lola."

"From their manner I think they do."

"Those kids out there behaving themselves?" He accepted a cup of coffee from Lola.

"Which reminds me," she cried. "that Chico!" She darted out and brought him in and stood him before Joe.

160

"What's he done?" Joe set his cup down and stooped to the boy's level.

"I sent him out to tell Mamá that your parents were here and he didn't do it."

"I forgot. Mamá told me to water my onions." Chico, with bowed head, twisted his fingers in embarrassment and looked to Margarita for sympathy. She smiled encouragement.

"Well, Lola, I don't think that's a capital offense. You'd surely not send him to jail for that," Joe told her.

At the mention of jail Chico broke away from Joe and ran to Margarita. She held him close.

"It showed disrespect to your mamá and papá," Lola insisted.

"Oh, they didn't give it a thought. They've put up with me for twenty-four years so they know a man often forgets. I think we should let him off this time."

"I might have known what you'd say."

"Well, Lola, we men have to hang together. Now I think he's entitled to some fruit or a cookie for being frightened half to death. What will it be, Chico?" He lowered the tray so the boy could make his selection and watched him as he left the room peeling a banana. "He's a cute kid," he said. "Lola and I may adopt him after we're married. Now, having done my duty to El Abrigo, I'd better get on my patrol."

"Joe, I've asked your parents for Sunday dinner. Can you make it, too?" Margarita asked.

"Sure, I'll be here," he promised as he went through the door. A moment later the clatter of his motorcycle broke the stillness of the afternoon.

Chapter 19

"Lola, did you hear that?" Margarita had aroused out of a sound sleep.

"What, Mamá?" Lola answered from the back bedroom.

"That scraping noise on the porch...there, do you hear it?"

"Yes, I'll call Anselmo."

"Perhaps you'd better." Margarita arose, and by the time she had slipped into a robe Lola was back with Anselmo.

"What's the matter?" he asked, sleepily.

"There's something on the porch. Wait, don't open the door yet. Let's go out the back way and come around to the front of the house. We can see what it is and have room to run if we have to," Lola whispered.

"I'm not afraid," Anselmo said and jerked the door open. A half-smothered moan reached his ears.

"It's a woman," he said.

"Let me rest here until morning, then I'll move on. I can go no farther tonight." she sobbed.

Anselmo looked back to Margarita. "Can she stay?"

"Of course, but she can't sit out there all night. It's too cold. Lola, help Anselmo bring her in while I light a lamp." Margarita went into the kitchen to get the lamp, and while she was fumbling around in the dark Lola joined her.

"Mamá, the woman is pregnant."

"Oh, no!"

"Yes, she is. And she's no tramp. Her clothes are good and she, well...she looks like a lady."

"Whatever her social standing she has to be helped. Where are the matches? I'll be glad if we ever get power all night long. This having the electricity cut off at midnight is ridiculous!"

Lola felt along the shelf. "Here, Mamá, here's a match." She shielded the sputtering flame while Margarita bared the lamp wick. It caught, the glass chimney was replaced, and Lola carried the lamp into the next room. The stranger was slumped in a chair and Anselmo was supporting her.

"She's in no condition to tell us anything tonight," Margarita observed. "Let's see if we can get her to my bed, Lola. Do you think we can lift her?"

"I doubt it, but we can try. Wait...there's someone at the door."

Before Lola could open it a voice called, "Margarita? Is anything wrong?"

"Frank, you're just in time to help us get this poor woman in bed."

He came in, looked at the woman, and asked, "Who is she?"

"We don't know. She asked if she could stay on the porch until morning, but she's ill—I couldn't leave her out there in the cold," Margarita said.

Frank shook his head. "I believe there is some

quality in you that attracts the unfortunate. Where do you want me to put her?"

"On my bed."

"No, Mamá, on mine. I can sleep anywhere. Bring her back here."

"Dr. Barrerra isn't in town, is he?" Frank asked.

"I haven't seen him," Margarita said.

"Tomorrow's his day," Lola told them.

"I'll watch for him in the morning and get him to make this his first call." Frank removed the woman's shoes from her sore and swollen feet. Carefully Margarita bathed them and put ointment on the blisters.

As soon as Frank left she and Lola took off the woman's dress and covered her with a blanket. They sat watching her for a few moments and then quietly left the room.

———————

"I wonder how our lady feels this morning." Lola swung her feet over the side of the hammock and yawned.

"Pretty stiff and sore, I surmise." Margarita finished dressing while Lola tiptoed to the door of her room to check.

The woman was asleep but kept moving as if in pain. When the fragrance of coffee began to permeate the air she roused and called, "Please...someone...where am I?"

Lola answered. "You're in the home of Señora Marquez."

164

Margarita came in, smiling. "We'll have the doctor stop on his way to the hotel where he has an office."

"Oh, no, please! I'll be all right after I rest for a while. I have no money to pay a doctor."

"The doctor must see your feet, and when he does I'm sure he'll insist you stay off them for a while. Now...would you like some coffee? Lola is bringing it now." The woman struggled to a sitting position and reached for the cup. Margarita left to check on breakfast preparations, and the doctor came while she was out.

"The Professor told me you had a late visitor. Where is she?" he asked. Lola led him back to the patient. When he came out later he asked for Margarita.

"I don't know how you do it, Señora, but you never miss. You've acquired another responsibility. This woman should not be on her feet for several weeks. What are you going to do with her?"

"Take care of her, of course."

"She has no money."

"I don't expect any."

"I know." The doctor sighed. "Lola, how about a cup of your coffee? I must plan our next move."

"Doctor, don't let this worry you. What's one more person in the house?"

"In this case, about six more burdens. I tell you what I think I'll do. I've dressed her feet as well as I can now, but I don't have the medication I need and Filomeno doesn't carry it."

"Have you had breakfast, Doctor?" Lola asked, handing him the coffee.

"Oh, yes, long ago, but I needed this. I didn't expect to be faced with such a problem as soon as I got here, so I didn't come fortified. Ah...here comes the Professor."

"How is the lady?" Frank asked.

"In a lot of pain. I was just telling Señora Marquez that she has a bed patient for a couple of weeks."

"Did you learn who she is, and where she came from, and why she was stumbling around at two o'clock in the morning? Where is her husband...or does she have one?"

"Yes, she talked quite freely. She's Californian by birth and left school to elope with this rascal to Tijuana where they had a church wedding before going on to Mexico City. After she became pregnant he decided he didn't want the responsibility of a family and taunted her with the fact that a church wedding isn't considered a legal union in this country. He refused to have a civil ceremony, so she left him."

"Where was she headed when she came here?"

"She was trying to get back home. She either lost or was robbed of her purse. Now, Margarita, I'm going to make this as easy on you as I can. I'll have her up as soon as I think it's safe. I'll go on down to the hotel and get an order off to Rudy for a prescription, but it won't get here until nine tonight. Then I'll come back and dress her feet. I'll show you how it's done so you can take care of them until I'm in this area again."

"Doctor, why not give me the order and let me drive in and get what you need?"

"But what about your classes?"

"I'll get someone to take over while I'm gone."

"Fine. Let me write this down and you can be on your way. I'm going to leave something for pain, Margarita. I know the woman is suffering. Give her this capsule; I'll see how she responds to it when I come back at noon."

A commotion on the patio announced the boys' rising, and Lola went out to investigate. The small, black heads were bent over their individual wash basins. It was Pablo's turn to draw water for the face washing, and Anselmo charged him with cheating him of his rightful share. When they sensed Lola's presence Anselmo calmed down, and Pablo added water to his bowl.

"Now brush your teeth and come to breakfast. Dorina has it ready," she told them and returned to the sick room. But peace was short lived and again it was Anselmo who broke it.

"Mamá," he yelled, "somebody's been using my toothpaste!"

Margarita answered the call. "Are you sure?"

"Yes, and I know who it was, too. Pablo!"

"Why do you accuse Pablo?"

"Because he looks sneaky."

"Do you have enough paste for this morning?"

"Yes."

"Then why are you fussing because someone used a little?"

"I don't want Pablo touching my things."

"I'll ask Pablo about it, but I don't think you should accuse your brother of taking your toothpaste."

"He's not my brother! He's just...just...accepted!"

167

"Well, so were you."

"I know, but I got here first."

"Quit arguing and come to the table. You'll be late for school if you don't hurry."

"Those boys!" Lola sighed when Margarita returned.

"I suppose it's normal for boys to spar like that. And yet, if one of them gets into trouble away from home they all rush to his assistance—with Anselmo in the lead."

"It was my Joe that straightened him out," Lola said proudly.

"Yes, Joe's been a big help." Margarita walked out to the patio and back again. "I feel so disorganized this morning, Lola. There's so much to do, and I don't know where to start. I think, though, that I'd better go into the village and get some material for gowns for our guest. I won't be gone long."

"Well, I hear you've done it again," was Henrietta's greeting as Margarita stepped into Señora Valdez' shop.

"You speak as if I'd committed a crime."

"I'm not sure that you haven't, burdening yourself with an ill, pregnant woman!"

"Poor thing, she really needs help."

"But it isn't your duty to take her in."

"Should I have turned her away?"

"You couldn't...you aren't made like that. And I wouldn't have you any other way." Henrietta smiled at her. "I came to get material for some dresses. You'll make them up for me, of course. You know what I like."

"Don't you want something different this time, Henrietta? We've used the same pattern for three years."

"Basically, I want the same style. If you'd like to add a new touch it's all right; use your own judgment."

"Elana, give Margarita the pieces I chose. . . and let her have whatever she needs for the sick woman and charge it to me. I have a feeling that she's here to buy something for the patient."

"No, Henrietta, I'll pay for this myself. I don't expect anyone else to share the expense."

"Elana, do as I say."

When she got home Margarita found the patient sitting up in bed talking with Lola. At Margarita's entrance she began to apologize.

"Don't give it another thought, Señora. . . ."

"Munoz. Estrella Munoz, but please call me Esta."

"Very well, Esta. Did Lola tell you that you must rest for two or three weeks?"

"Oh, no! I cannot accept so much."

"You must rest. Dr. Barrerra will tell you when you can leave."

Chapter 20

Before the week had passed Margarita had become "mamá" to Esta, also.

"Let me do something," she begged. "I can't sit idle while the rest of you are busy."

"Perhaps you can help me with the sewing. I have a lot for ladies of the village and all of Lola's dresses to make."

So Margarita fitted the garments and operated the machine while Esta finished them.

"Well, Esta," she said one morning, "we've emptied the chest of everything except Lola's trousseau. Shall we start on that?"

"Yes, the great day isn't too far off."

"No girl in Alhaja ever had so many pretty dresses all at once," Lola gloated as Margarita spread the materials out and began measuring. Her delight was boundless when Margarita finally cut into the length of satin that was to be the wedding gown. Although it could have been made on the sewing machine, Esta insisted on doing it by hand and spent many hours stitching the garment.

"Who's going to look after the Professor while I'm away?" Lola asked as she pressed one of her new dresses.

"I suppose I will," Margarita replied.

"Why can't Esta?"

"That's an idea. Would you like to, Esta?"

"I'd like to help any way I can."

"Well, that's the solution. Señor Faz will pay you a small wage. You'd better go over with Lola each morning until you learn the routine."

"It won't take long to learn—he isn't hard to please."

After the third day Esta worked alone while Lola spent her time getting her future home ready for occupancy.

One day Esta was gone so long that Margarita became uneasy and walked over to check on her. She found her, mop in hand, completely engrossed in a book. Esta looked up when she heard Margarita's step.

"I was afraid you were ill, Esta," Margarita explained her intrusion. "It's almost lunchtime."

"Have I been here that long? But do you know what I found here on the table? A Book of Mormon!"

"Oh? What do you know about it?"

"Not nearly enough. I was studying it with a friend when I left California. I'm sorry I didn't finish my work first. I'll get the Professor's lunch and clean the house later."

When Frank came home at noon his meal was on the table and Esta was mopping the patio. She could hardly wait until he had finished eating before she approached him.

"Señor Faz," she began, eyes shining, "I see you have a Book of Mormon."

"It isn't mine. It belongs to my friend, John Acosta."

"Of Mexico City?"

"Yes, do you know him?"

"No, but one of my neighbors in the City did. She thinks he's an exceptional man."

"He's all of that—a fine man, but a deluded one."

"Deluded?"

"Yes. John has a good education and a good mind, but do you know that he believes that book was translated miraculously from gold plates delivered to a farm boy by an angel?"

"What's so strange about that?"

"There are no miracles today!"

"No miracles today? Look at me! A miracle is being performed in my body—the creation of another person. What directs certain cells to amass in one area to form the eyes, the hands and feet, and all the other parts of that small body? And birth is the greatest miracle of all."

"Birth is the natural consequence of a natural act," Frank maintained.

"And nature, as the nuns taught us in school, is God at work in his world today."

"I still can't believe that God spoke to a boy," Frank said, ignoring her comment.

"According to the Bible God spoke to men—it is filled with accounts of such conversations."

"That was an entirely different situation. Civilization was in its infancy and those people needed the guidance they got from inspiration."

"Isn't that rather like saying people don't need to be fed after they're grown...that they should be able to

172

exist on the food given them when they're children?
The word of God is spiritual food, and we always need
it. If the time ever comes that we reject the word of
God, civilization will die."

"Are you a member of that church?"

"No, my husband wouldn't let me join, but if I ever
have another opportunity I'm going to."

All the preliminaries for Lola's wedding had been
cared for, and the day for the ceremony had arrived.
The entire Marquez household was up before sunrise.
The boys ate breakfast in pajamas in order to keep
their clothes fresh for church. Margarita and Esta took
Lola in charge.

"I'm nervous, Mamá," Lola confided.

"It's a big step—one that will change your life—but
as long as you and Joe love each other, you can adjust."

"I hope I can please Joe's mother."

"Joe is the one you're to please. I'm glad you're going
into your own home and won't have to share that of
your in-laws. I wish the ceremony wasn't going to be
performed at the church door."

"It's the custom, Mamá,"

"I know—but I still don't like it. If Joe's parents
weren't paying for it I would insist that the marriage
service be held inside the church. Here you are, a
lovely bride, having to stand in the doorway while the
priest hears your vows."

"How were you married?"

"In a civilized manner! Mariano waited at the altar

173

with his best man, and I went up the aisle to him on my father's arm."

"But the altar is sacred!" Lola objected.

"So is marriage!" Margarita countered.

Grant and Pasquelo drove down for the occasion and went to Frank's house to wait out the time. Shortly before they were due at the church Margarita saw Joe pass the house to join them.

"How long will you be away, Lola? Did Joe get an extension or are you still limited to three days?"

"Just three days, Esta. It's all we can afford. Hotels are expensive. Besides, Joe says it wouldn't be right to keep the Professor's car any longer."

"He's right. It was kind of Señor Faz to lend it."

"Now, Lola," Margarita gave the veil a final twitch, "you'd better loop the end of your train over your arm until you get to the church. I hope the Morales get a good look at you, for they'll never see a lovelier bride. They'll understand why their Joe wouldn't look at another girl."

When the women appeared on the porch the men crossed over to join them. Joe's eyes shone when he stepped up and held out his hand to Lola. She put hers into it, and they walked up the road to the church. Grant took Margarita's arm while Esta and Frank herded the boys ahead of them to meet with the gathering of family and friends.

The Morales, affluent by village standards, had made every effort to make their only child's wedding a memorable occasion. An elaborate reception followed the nuptial mass, and the crowd moved to their home to spend the rest of the day in celebration. Margarita didn't stay long since duty called her home. She found her charges and Pasquelo at the dinner table. Grant was in the garden.

"Didn't you go to the reception?" she asked.

"No, such gatherings bore me, especially when I know so few people. I've been looking at your garden. It's more fruitful than mine."

"Well, I have eight gardeners, each vying with the others for production. This plot supplies us with most of our food."

They strolled back to the house and paused at the well.

"Margarita, why do you have this well when you have water piped into the house?"

"The well was here when we bought the place, but because we were at the foot of the hill at the lower end of the valley my husband was afraid the water wouldn't be pure enough for drinking, so he had water brought in. We use the well for the laundry, the animals, and the garden when necessary."

"Well, it's good to have both sources. Now. . . let's go up to the hotel for lunch."

"Should I. . . with Lola gone?"

"Esta can manage, and here comes Frank. Let's requisition his services. Frank, can you supervise this place while I take Señora Marquez to the hotel for lunch?"

"Of course. Henrietta has a good menu today. Go and enjoy your meal."

The sound of muffled groans awoke Margarita. She rolled out of bed and put her feet on the floor in one continuous movement.

"Yes, Esta?"

"The pains are very bad. I think it's time."

Margarita ran to the dormitory and awakened Anselmo. "Go get Lola...quickly," she ordered. "Tell her I need her help." When he was on his way, she returned to Esta's bedside.

When Lola arrived she went directly to Esta's room and asked, "How long have you had pains?"

"They started about an hour ago, but they're getting worse."

"And they'll get even worse." Lola was short on comfort.

"Had I better send for Señora Menchaca?" Margarita asked.

"No, I can do all that she does. I've helped Juanita have half a dozen babies."

"Is there anything I can do?"

"Yes, you can get the baby's things ready."

Margarita got the box of clothes and set it on the kitchen table, then stood by and suffered vicariously with Esta. Lola was stoic through it all. "Women have babies every day, Mamá," she said, matter-of-factly. "Don't worry so much."

"Are you sure I shouldn't go for Señora Menchaca?"

"And pay her five pesos for what I can do for nothing? I can handle this better alone. Go get dressed—you're still in your gown."

Before she returned she heard Esta give a sharp cry.

When she returned to the back bedroom Lola was holding the baby by its feet and slapping it to make it gasp for breath. When it had cooperated she handed it to Margarita, saying, "Here, you take it so I can look after Esta."

"Oh, it's a little girl!" Margarita cried as she reached for it.

"Is it? I didn't have time to notice," Lola said and turned back to the bed.

Joe came in from his run that afternoon and Lola returned home with him. Later in the day Frank came in, bearing a sheaf of calla lilies.

"Flowers for the new arrival," he said, handing them to Margarita. "Am I permitted to see the miracle?"

"Yes, come in. Esta, your daughter has received her first flowers from a gentleman. Aren't they lovely?"

"They're beautiful! Thank you so much, Señor Faz." She touched one of the flowers lightly and looked from the blossoms to the sleeping baby. "I've been trying to think of a name for her, and you have helped me decide. I'll call her 'Calla.'"

Chapter 21

"Isn't Mamá home yet?" Lola poured herself a cup of coffee and sat down to watch as Esta pinned a fresh diaper on Calla.

"No, I don't expect her before Sunday. It's good that she can spend this time with her son."

"She must be enjoying herself." Lola sipped her coffee thoughtfully for a moment, then asked, "The boys give you any trouble this week?"

"Not really. I had to call on Frank yesterday. Andy was acting up."

"I'm sorry I couldn't spend more time with you while Mamá is away, but Joe was on short patrol and you know what that means. If he has time for only a sandwich he wants me at home. He'll be gone for the next two nights so I'll stay with you. Are you making any Christmas plans for the boys?"

"Just a dinner. I wish we could have the kind of Christmas we used to have at home."

"Tell me about it."

"We always decorated the house upstairs and down. We'd have tree-trimming parties and go from house to house helping each other. We made most of our gifts because we didn't have a lot of money, but I think they're the nicest kind anyway. If you go to the trouble to make a gift it shows that you care a lot. As we

178

finished making our presents, we wrapped them and put them under the tree. Then on Christmas morning we gathered in the living room and opened them. I've missed that since I left home."

"We don't do that here. Our children get their gifts on the sixth of January—the day of the Feast of the Kings."

"I know the custom, but I like the California way better. I think I've given the boys time enough to get ready for bed, so I'll go in and read to them for a while. Will you hold Calla?"

"Of course. . . . Come here, beautiful. Let's go in and listen to the story. What are you reading to them?" Lola balanced the baby over her shoulder and followed Esta into the dormitory.

"*The Other Wise Man.* Frank got it in the last shipment of books. As soon as I finish this we'll take up the Bible Christmas story, then the one in the Book of Mormon."

The boys were in their hammocks, chattering like squirrels. At Esta's entrance a warning "shush" from Anselmo quieted them, and they all turned to face her. After fifteen minutes of reading she closed the book and told the boys goodnight.

"If we could only manage a small gift for each one," Esta yearned as she closed the door.

Margarita came home on Sunday and again took command. Esta voiced her wish for Christmas gifts for the boys a few days later.

"If it's nothing more than special cookies. . .something they don't have every day, something to set Christmas apart."

"I'll think about it," Margarita promised, "but we can't ask our sponsors to do more than they're already doing. And if Señor Bera didn't bring us chickens and eggs we'd have a hard time getting by."

"It seems a shame to me that there isn't more enthusiasm about the holidays."

"The villagers will have the Posadas as usual."

"Yes, I know, and there will be a midnight mass on the twenty-fifth. But what small child understands all that? As soon as Calla is old enough she's going to be told all the wonder and mystery of the season. I want her to bubble over with excitement when she hears of the baby in the manger, of the shepherds on the hill, and of the Magi and their gifts. That reminds me; while you were away I've been reading to the boys each night. I've finished *The Other Wise Man*, and tonight I want to share Luke's story of the nativity . . . if it's all right with you."

"Of course it is, but what prompted you to start that?"

"Christmas. I can't help thinking of all the boys have missed."

"Now, Esta. . . ."

"I know what you're going to say. And I agree—the boys *are* better off than they've ever been before. They have food, clothes, and a good place to sleep. But life should be more than that. I remember when I was small how thrilled I was when my mother praised me for a good grade on a test paper, how sure I was of

180

comfort and understanding if I failed. But these children have no one to run to for sympathy in their disappointments."

"Esta, the boys know that I'm available for all of their needs."

"I know, Mamá, we're both available, but I doubt that we're deeply concerned. I was thinking the other night when Pablo was ill...if he died, who would grieve for him? Who would really care? Oh, I'm sure we'd give him the best funeral we could afford, and we would go to the cemetery on the Day of the Dead and burn a candle on his grave. But no one would treasure special moments spent with him. Some other boy would soon fill his hammock and our thoughts. With all we've tried to give them here they've missed the greatest of earthly gifts—a home and parents."

"I believe I'm doing all I can, Esta. However, if you'll tell me where I'm failing I'll try to correct it." There was a hint of resentment in Margarita's voice.

"I don't mean to criticize...and I don't think anyone could have done more. It's just that Christmas means so much to me, and I want these boys to know the real joys of childhood. If Angela pays me for making her dress as she promised, I'll have a little money. I think I'll divide it between Calla and the boys. It's just as well that she begins sharing now."

"Well, don't do any buying yet, Esta. Let me talk with Frank. Perhaps we can work out something."

"But I should know right away...with Christmas so near."

"The children get their gifts next month, Esta, on the sixth. It's the village custom."

Margarita and Frank had several consultations during the week, but Esta was not told the outcome. She and Lola were surprised when Margarita returned to Mexico on the Monday before Christmas.

"What about dinner, Mamá? I thought you would be here to eat with us."

"Don't worry, girls, you know I won't spend Christmas away from you and the boys. I'll be here in time to help prepare the meal."

"I simply don't understand her," Esta said as Grant's car rolled onto the road. "I'm sure she's in love with Señor Bera, and love makes a person do strange things, but I don't think that even romance should have this effect on a mature woman."

"Joe's been acting peculiar, too. I don't know what's happening to everybody," Lola said.

Esta had a note from Margarita two days later telling her to be sure that the boys' good clothes were in order.

"That means they have to go to midnight mass," she concluded.

Margarita came home on the twenty-fourth.

"I was afraid you wouldn't make it," Esta told her.

"I promised that I wouldn't be away from you on Christmas Day. Now I have a surprise for you. We're all going to Señor Bera's house for the holiday. That's what has kept me in Mexico City so much lately—making plans and preparing for the celebration."

182

"Really? Then the boys will get to see the beautiful decorations!"

"Yes, we'll have supper at the ranch tonight and sight-see later. Now we'll have to hurry and get things together."

"I wish Lola could be with us."

"She will be. Joe's bringing her down in a little while."

"This is the nicest treat the boys could possibly have," Esta exulted.

When Lola joined them the entire El Abrigo staff and residents piled into the two cars and set out for the Bera ranch.

Pasquelo had stayed at home to help the servants with the last-minute arrangements. It was growing dark when he heard the cars stop on the driveway, and as the door opened to admit the guests he pressed a button lighting up the huge Christmas tree that filled one corner of the room. There were cries of delight as the boys crowded close to see this marvel. Esta wept.

"I wish Joe could see this," Lola lamented. "It is so beautiful!"

"Joe *has* seen it, Lola; he helped us set it up. He'll be with us tomorrow."

Grant allowed time for admiration of the tree, then called them all in to supper. The Acostas joined them at the table.

"Now as soon as we've eaten we'll drive around and see the town," Grant promised.

It was an evening to remember. The Acosta car was added to the tour, and for two hours they drove through the City and finally to the top of a hill where they looked down on the breathtaking view. At one place shepherds sat around a fire with their sheep lying nearby. At another, duplicate characters looked up to an angel hovering in the air above them. At still another place the Magi kept their eyes on a glittering star while their camels plodded across the desert. Grant and his guests lingered in silence until the cold mountain air forced them back into the cars.

Calla was put to bed as soon as they returned to the ranch, then Esta joined the rest of the group in front of the television set. At the conclusion of the program Margarita announced bedtime for her charges. There was a clamor of protest; none of the boys wanted the day to end.

"We haven't had our story yet," Anselmo said. "You promised us a good one tonight, Señora Munoz."

"That was before I knew we were coming here for Christmas," Esta hedged.

"Go ahead," Grant urged. "We need a Christmas story to crown the evening."

"Well," Esta began self-consciously, "I didn't expect this audience, but I'll do my best. Now part of this story is true, part I made up.

"A long time ago, long before the Spaniards came, this land was the home of many people. It was a good land. The soil was rich, and the farms produced huge harvests. The mountains held gold and silver, and the people were very prosperous. You would think that with all this that God gave them they would have been especially good, but they weren't—at least most of

184

them weren't. There were some who tried to do right, and there were ministers who went about telling of the mercy and love of God and warning them of severe punishment if they didn't repent and accept Christ, for they had been taught about Jesus. But the wicked people just laughed and went on in the same old way. Now there was a prophet named Samuel who preached against their evildoing in such a manner that it made them angry, and they tried to kill him. But he ran from the city and escaped.

"Just outside the town there lived a widow with her blind son. He was about as big as Chico. They had a small farm like Mamá's, and when Samuel saw their little house he asked if he could hide there for a while. The widow said, 'yes,' and let him come in.

"After supper Samuel told them of the prophecies concerning the birth of Christ. He told them that there would be a night without darkness and that a new star would appear. And he said all this would happen in five years.

"The little blind boy listened to every word, and when Samuel spoke of the star he cried out, 'When the star shines I'll see it!' His mother tried to discourage the thought because she couldn't see how anyone born blind could ever see.

"Well, the five years passed. The wicked people became even worse and passed a law that all those who believed in Samuel's prophecy would be executed on a certain day. You can imagine how the believers felt. One of their ministers went out into the woods to pray about this, and as he knelt a voice told him not to worry, for that very night the star would shine.

"He ran back to the city and told the people of his experience, but some of them didn't believe him. They thought he was just trying to postpone the death of the believers. Then as the day drew to a close, the sun went down as it always had, but the sky remained as bright as at noon. Everyone was too excited to go to bed and wandered about, afraid of what was to come.

"All the next day the little boy sat at the window and kept asking his mother if it was night. 'As soon as it gets dark and the star shines I shall see it,' he said.

" 'I wish you weren't so sure,' his mother said, but he continued to say, 'I'll see the star.'

"After supper a large crowd gathered at the widow's house to discuss what had happened the night before and to listen again as the minister told them of the Christ. The boy, still sitting at the window, startled the people by suddenly crying out, 'There is the star! I see it! I see the star!'

"Everyone rushed out of the house and looked up. There, just above the cottage roof, a new star glittered and the boy said, 'I have seen his star!' "

The children turned from Esta to look at the star-topped tree.

"Yes," she said, following their movement, "that's why we put a star at the top of the tree—to commemorate the appearance of that first Christmas star. And the beautiful tree symbolizes the eternal life I've told you of."

"Thank you, Esta," Grant said. "You've given us an inspiring thought. Now, Frank, if you'll help John take the ladies over to his house we'll get the beds ready here. Then both of you are to return for the night. We'll see you ladies at breakfast."

Frank took Margarita and Esta in the front seat with him. Lola, Dorina, and her children occupied the back seats. The overflow went in the Acosta car.

The guests chorused their good-nights to Grant and the boys as the cars moved off to join the traffic on the highway.

"Esta, have you ever thought of writing?" Frank asked.

"Oh, no, Señor Faz. I could never do that."

"I'm not so sure. You certainly have a flair for storytelling. Tonight's tale was very interesting."

"It's as old as time, Professor."

"The Nativity story, yes, but you gave it a new twist. That was quite ingenious."

"Except for the characters of mother and son, the story is not original. You'll find the account in the Book of Mormon," she told him.

"That I've got to see!" he said.

Although it was almost midnight when he reached home the next night Frank looked for the Book of Mormon to verify Esta's claim for the base of her story. But then he remembered that he had urged Margarita to take it home and read it. Why hadn't he borrowed another copy from John, he asked himself. Perhaps Margarita hadn't gone to bed and he could get the book again. He stepped outside and looked next door, then sighed with relief when he saw her closing the dormitory door after her nightly check. He crossed over and made his request.

"I'll be glad to get it for you." She stepped inside and came back with it. "Let me know what you find out."

"You're interested, too?"

"Well, it seems almost impossible. . . ." She avoided giving a direct answer.

"It seems so to me, too. Good-night, Margarita. It *has* been a merry Christmas, hasn't it?"

"It surely has, Frank."

He moved his chair close to the lamp and sat down with the book. "I wonder where I'll find that," he mused. "If I can think of the name of the chap who did the prophesying. . . John, Matthew, Peter—those were in the Bible stories. It was a common name. . .ah, Samuel, that's it! I should find him listed in the index." He turned to the back of the book and ran down the listing. "Sacraments, Saints, Sam, Samuel. . .all right, old fellow, let's see what you have to say." He found the page indicated and read the predictions of calamities to come unless there was a return to righteousness. It seemed an endless number, but at last he came to the subject he sought.

Behold, I give you a sign: five years more will come, and, behold, then will come the Son of God to redeem all of those who shall believe on his name.

. . .This will I give you as a sign of his coming; for behold, there shall be great lights in heaven, insomuch that in the night before he comes, there shall be no darkness. . . .

There shall be one day and a night and a day, as if it were one day and there were no night; and this shall be to you a sign; for

188

you shall know of the rising of the sun and also its setting.

You shall know of a surety that there shall be two days and a night; nevertheless the night shall not be darkened, and it shall be the night before he is born.

And, behold, there shall be a new star arise, such a one as you have never beheld; and this also shall be a sign to you.

Frank read the rest of the page and, finding that there was the end of the prophecy concerning the Nativity, put the book aside.

"John said this was the work of an uneducated farm boy, but no unlearned man wrote that. Someone somewhere along the line had something pretty special. Not that I believe a word of it," he hastened to assure himself, "and it irritates me that Isobel and John are so gullible."

He arose and dressed for bed.

"I'd better try to read this as I promised John I would." As he reached for the book it slipped from his hand and fell open at the index. "Wow! Look how many times this refers to the 'record.' There must be a hundred." He glanced down the column and read, "Many kept that are particular and large...hidden by Ammoron...to shine forth out of darkness...Mormon seals up. I know I'm going to be bored, but I might as well get at this. I'm glad the electricity is off...gives me a good excuse for not reading long." He carried the lamp to the bedside table, settled back against his pillows, and resigned himself to his task.

"I'd better jot down some notes. I want to record any discrepancies." He arose, got pencil and paper, then went back to bed. He had not read far when he came to the account of the killing of Laban by Nephi—a murderer who claimed he had been directed by God to commit the crime! Just wait until he confronted John with this! Wasn't one of the commandments "Thou shalt not kill"? And yet, a little nagging thought kept intruding. When he was reading the Bible he wondered at the many times the Israelites were commanded to kill their enemies, to "destroy them utterly and show no mercy." Of course that was to keep the chosen people from falling into the idolatrous practices of the conquered foe. What reason did the Book of Mormon give? He turned back and read, " 'Behold, the Lord slayeth the wicked to bring forth his righteous purposes.' Same reason when you boil it down," he admitted grudgingly. He decided not to mention this to John, after all. Skipping from one page to another he paused when he read, "And we became exceedingly rich in gold and silver—and also in iron, and copper, brass and steel."

At last he had found something! Gold and silver he had to accept, for the Spaniards discovered temples and palaces containing these metals. . . but iron? John said the archaeologists flouted the idea that the natives had any knowledge of iron or the smelting of it. And hadn't the experts agreed that the carving on walls and stelae had been done with stone chisels? Of course, John didn't agree with them, but then he was no authority. Here was a mistake this so-called prophet had made. Frank reached for his pencil and paper. As he did so the book fell and a newspaper clipping came out. He picked it up and read:

190

Yesterday's Fancy Today's Fact

There has been a lot of controversy in archaeological circles as to whether or not the Pre-Columbian Indian had any knowledge of the use of iron. The Mormons claim that the ancients had iron, steel, and brass, as well as silver and gold about which there has never been any question. So far, nothing has been found to support their assertion as no remains of iron objects have been discovered. Archaeologists have used this to discount the idea of iron smelting, although admitting that any tools made of this metal would have rusted away after such a length of time.

Now score one for the Mormons. Recently there has been uncovered at Uaxactun a jar containing a quantity of iron oxide. Uaxactun is the site of some interesting Maya ruins in Guatemala.

Frank used the clipping to mark his place, slammed the book shut, and dropped it to the floor. He looked ruefully at the untouched notepaper.

"Time wasted," he said to himself. A glance at the clock told him the hour—4:30. "That can't be! I know I haven't read that long. The clock must have stopped yesterday afternoon." He held it to his ear. It was ticking away dutifully. He blew out the light and lay back.

Chapter 22

After celebrating the Feast of the Kings on January 6 the villagers settled back into peaceful lethargy. Pasquelo had come down that morning bringing gifts for the boys and Calla.

"Where's Señor Bera?" Margarita asked.

"He's at home. He wants to buy some land and he had to see the owner today," he explained. "Well," he said, looking at his wristwatch, "I'd better get back to the hotel if I'm to catch my bus."

"You aren't staying over until tomorrow?" Margarita asked.

"No, Mamá, I have a date tonight."

"The bus doesn't come until three o'clock, Pasquelo," his mother said hopefully.

"There's a tourist bus due at nine. Henry thinks I can get a ride in on that."

So Margarita walked with him to the hotel and watched until he had boarded the bus. As it pulled away Henrietta called her in.

"Haven't seen you in two days," she said.

"No, the place has been upside-down ever since Christmas. I'm glad the holidays are over. I don't like the confusion. I doubt that I could ever live in a large city."

"Were you thinking of leaving us?"

"Of course not! I just wonder how Pasquelo adjusted so quickly to life in the city."

"He's young and eager for adventure. You lived in Laredo for a number of years, and it isn't exactly a village. You didn't have any trouble adjusting then, did you?"

"I didn't need to. I was born there. Pasquelo has spent all of his life in the valley, yet I believe he feels more relaxed in Grant's home than in mine."

"Pasquelo has always been a man's man, hasn't he? As I remember, he was forever tagging at Mariano's heels."

"Yes, he was always devoted to his father. I'm surprised and a little pained that he can replace him so easily." Margarita's voice trembled and tears came to her eyes.

"Stop that this minute! You're feeling sorry for yourself, and Grant has not replaced you nor Mariano. If Pasquelo's absence affects you so, why not bring him home?"

"He would never forgive me...and I couldn't forgive myself if I deprived him of the education he's getting. I just miss him, and he's growing away from me."

"He'd do that if he never left Alhaja. Every young thing leaves the nest. Maybe you just need to get away from the village for a while. Let's take the nine o'clock bus in the morning and spend the day in Cuernavaca. We'll visit the shops, and you can get some new ideas for dressmaking. Then we'll see a matinee, and come home on the midnight bus."

"How will Henry manage without you?"

"One of the girls can help out for a day—Miranda is pretty bright. Henry will be all right. We'll make this a day to remember!"

Esta tiptoed past Calla's crib and out to the kitchen.

"Julia, did Margarita tell you when she would be home? She didn't come in at all last night."

"She must have stayed at the hotel, for if Henrietta hadn't gotten in you could hear Henry roaring from one end of the village to the other. He wants her in sight all the time!"

"Have you roused the boys?"

"Yes, they're washing up. Ah...there comes the Señora now!"

"We were beginning to worry!" Esta met Margarita at the door. "Come in and I'll fix your breakfast."

"No, I ate breakfast with Henry and Henrietta."

"You can at least have a cup of coffee with me," Esta coaxed. "You and Henrietta must have made a day of it."

"We did, and I enjoyed every minute of it. Now I'm ready to settle down again. Henrietta bought material for six new dresses and, under protest, a new pattern. I picked up several remnants for Calla. She's outgrowing everything she has. Henrietta isn't in a hurry for her clothes, so let's make Calla's before something else comes in. Is she still asleep?"

"Yes, she was up playing with the boys until late and then was too excited to go to sleep. I'll be with you as soon as I get the professor's breakfast and set his place in order."

Margarita had just pinned a pattern to a piece of material when she heard a car drive up and stop.

"Can you see who's coming, Esta?"

"It's the Bera car."

Pasquelo entered the room like a gulf storm.

"Hi, Mamá, you know why we're here?"

"To see me, I hope."

"We've come to take you into the City for a few days. There's a show Dad wants you to see."

"Where is Grant?"

"He stopped to talk with the professor. They're coming in now. You'll go with us, won't you?"

"Pasquelo, I'm not prepared to go anywhere."

"You don't need any preparation, Margarita. We'll have supper at the ranch and drive out afterward. Pasquelo suggested a picnic in the Teotihuacan area tomorrow....It seems he once saw a group of picnickers out there. We'll see the native dances in the evening. How about it?" Grant urged.

"Of course you can go," Esta encouraged her. "You need to get away once in a while."

"But I just got home after being away all day," Margarita reminded them.

"That doesn't count. I'll pack your bag while you change," Esta said.

"I'm away too much as it is....I don't feel right about leaving you with all the responsibility."

"I'll call on Frank if I have any trouble," Esta assured her.

"Here, wear this pink dress I made for you last week. It's the most becoming thing you have...and you'd better take your pink sweater. You'll need it if you're out late. Now forget about us, and enjoy your visit."

"Shall we drive around for a while?" Grant asked after dinner.

"That would be nice. It's a lovely evening."

"I left the car out front. Pasquelo, are you coming with us?"

"No, Dad, Beaney's coming over."

"Okay, have fun." Grant picked up Margarita's sweater and ushered her to the door. For an hour or more they drove through the residential district of the City. As Grant turned the car toward the downtown area he asked, "Has Pasquelo spoken to you about going to college in the States?"

"No! Why would he want to do a thing like that? We have just as good schools here as they have north of the border."

"I know that, and so does he, but I think he wants to try his wings. Isobel has talked a lot about her college years and has a history of them in pictures. It has aroused his interest."

"What college did she attend?"

"Her church school in Iowa—Graceland, I think it's called."

"I never heard of it."

"Neither did I until Pasquelo began talking about it and wanting to go there."

"How do you feel about it?"

"How I feel has nothing to do with the question. That's your decision—and his. John says that it's a good school, and that a young person couldn't have a better environment."

"I don't know, Grant. I'll have to think about it."

"You do that. Now what do you want to do next?"

"Let's go sit on a park bench and watch the people pass by."

"Is that your idea of entertainment?"

"Don't you find it interesting to study faces?"

"Some faces, perhaps, but I doubt that you'd be able to notice anything in the park except beggars, shoeshine boys, lottery ticket and chewing gum salesmen. I'd love to indulge you in such a simple pleasure, but I'm sure you wouldn't be amused. Let's drive out toward Xochmilco instead."

"I haven't been there in years."

"We'll come out some Sunday and spend the day." They rode on in silence for some time, then Grant reached over and took her hand. "Margarita, we're no longer children," he began. "I think we've wasted enough time. You know I love you. . . ."

There was a scarcely audible murmur of denial.

"I'm sorry—that wasn't how I planned to do it. I'm going to take you back to the ranch where I can propose properly." He turned at the next intersection and headed home. On the mantel was a note from Pasquelo: "Gone to Beaney's. Be back early."

"Is he usually out late?" Margarita asked anxiously.

"He's perfectly safe—believe me. Now let's talk

about us. When I told you awhile ago that I loved you, I didn't hear an expression either of pleasure or interest. I'm not a rich man, but I can make life easier for you and give you much that can make it worth while. I'm not going to accept a refusal. I've almost worn the wheels off my car running down to Alhaja, knowing all the time that after I arrived I'd never have you to myself for a minute. I could do no more than shake your hand, wondering how it would be to take you in my arms. . . ."

"Why don't you find out, Grant?"

The Marquez rings were transferred to Margarita's right hand, and when she went home Sunday a diamond flashed from her left ring finger. She tried to disguise her new happiness, but Grant's air of proud possession would have announced the engagement had there been no ring.

Lola was putting a bandage on Adolph's knee when the two came in. One look and she made a flying leap to Margarita.

"Oh, Mamá, I've prayed for this. The Virgin has answered my prayers!"

Esta and the boys heard the commotion and crowded in to learn its cause. By nightfall the entire village had the news.

"How soon is the wedding to be?" Henrietta asked.

"We haven't discussed that yet, but it won't be for some time," Margarita replied.

"That's what you think," Grant contradicted. "I've waited too long already."

As the dining room began filling the two moved to the patio. "I have so many loose ends, Grant. I didn't realize it until I got to thinking. . . after I went to bed last night."

"Well, start gathering those loose ends."

"And the two little boys. I've adopted them. I'd have to take them with me."

"I understand. I'll give you time to do whatever you think has to be done, then you're coming home to the ranch. If Pasquelo goes north to school he'll leave in August, and I'd like to have him here for the ceremony."

Chapter 23

"Señora Marquez, do you have room for another stray?" Joe stepped onto the porch leading a small boy. "He spent the night at the base of the shrine at the hotel and got rained on. He's soaking wet and seems to have a cold."

"Of course; let me have him. Why, he's running a fever." The child stumbled and she stooped to pick him up.

"Let me have him, Mamá. I'll give him a bath and get him into dry clothes. He's shaking all over... poor little mite." Esta took him to the bathroom where she filled a small tub with warm water and put the child into it. But he would have toppled over if she had not supported him. When he was dressed in clean pajamas she placed him in the hammock in the front room.

He lay in a semi-stupor the rest of the day, refusing everything except water. Lola came to see him and suggested several medications, none of which he could keep down. As night fell he became restless and frequently cried. Both Margarita and Esta hovered over him until dawn.

"I'm afraid he has pneumonia," Margarita confided to Frank when he came in the next morning to ask about him.

"I'll drive into Cuernavaca and see if Dr. Barrerra

will prescribe something for him," he volunteered. "Why don't you let the boys take turns rocking the hammock? He seems quieter when it's in motion."

"I think I will. Esta and I were up all night and we're exhausted."

The boys were pressed into service and rotated every half hour. When Frank returned he brought the doctor with him.

"I'm sorry we had to disturb you, Doctor, but we've tried every remedy we know without one bit of success."

"That's all right, Margarita. I deserve this for not taking up a less demanding and more remunerating profession—such as house painting or plumbing. Where is the child? I understand he's another stray."

"Yes, he came yesterday."

"Do you know what I think, Margarita? I think the surrounding villagers since learning of El Abrigo drop their bush babies off here knowing they'll be cared for."

"You may be right. It seems to me that for every one we place we get a replacement almost immediately."

"Well, let me see the patient." Dr. Barrerra spent some time with him. "I'm concerned about this one. He's a very sick little boy. Our first job is to reduce that fever."

"I was afraid he might have pneumonia," Margarita ventured.

"There is some congestion. Let me see if I brought...yes, here it is. Frank gave me a fairly accurate description of his condition so I think I came prepared." He gave an injection and stood looking down at the small form, and again applied the stethoscope. "I'm not too sure of pulling this one through. He's terribly undernourished. I'll stay up at the hotel so I can check on him during the next twenty-four hours. Send for me if you need me."

Anselmo had taken his turn at swinging the hammock and had come in several times to stare at the newcomer.

"He's so little," he said as Margarita stood beside him. "Is he going to die?"

"I hope not, Anselmo, but he's very sick."

"I wonder why people have kids if they don't want them."

"I wonder, too." Margarita put an arm around his shoulders and together they continued their vigil.

"Mamá, he looks just like my little brother, Bito."

"Why, Anselmo, you never mentioned him before. Where is he?"

"Dead! That man killed him! He was little and sick and hungry and he cried!" There was a lot of pent-up bitterness in his voice. It was a struggle for him to speak, but it seemed he had to talk. "We hadn't had anything to eat all day, and Bito cried because he was hungry. And that devil took him by his feet and threw him against the wall, and Bito cried out for me, and his blood ran down onto the floor." His eyes were shut tight against his suffering and his body shook with his sobs. Margarita held him close, her tears giving her the relief the boy denied himself. Finally he became calm and for a moment hid his face against Margarita's breast, then turned back to the hammock.

"Mamá, if he lives can we call him Bito?"

"Of course," she agreed readily. "Now you've been here long enough. Let Adolph relieve you."

"No, I want to stay." So all afternoon Anselmo stood watch and could hardly be persuaded to leave his post to eat. The child's illness had disrupted the routine and supper was late. It was growing dark when Anselmo returned to the front room after eating. He bent over the baby and suddenly called to Margarita. "Mamá, come quick! Bito's got red spots on his face!"

Margarita and Esta both rushed into the room and examined the boy.

"What do you think, Esta?"

"I don't know, Mamá."

"I'm going for the doctor," Anselmo said and was out of the house before anyone thought to send him.

"It could be the measles. Have you had them, Mamá?"

"I don't know, I don't remember. Are they contagious?"

"Very." The women looked at each other.

"Every boy has been exposed," Margarita mourned.

"I'd better get Calla out of the house. I'm sure Lola will take care of her for me. I'll be right back." Esta hastily gathered up Calla's clothes and set out, meeting the doctor on the way.

"His entire body is covered with red spots, Doctor," Margarita greeted him.

A brief examination confirmed Esta's suspicions. Dr.

Barrerra looked around at the boys standing in awestruck silence.

"Well, Margarita, you've done it again. I thought taking a pregnant woman into your home had to be your crowning achievement, but you've beat your own record. Do you realize that we have a dozen possible cases of measles, unless some of these youngsters are immune?"

"Oh, no," Margarita groaned.

One after another of the boys succumbed to the illness. Anselmo refused at first to give up and stayed near Bito's hammock, but at last he was forced to retire to his own.

Frank took Margarita's message to Grant. The wedding would have to be postponed indefinitely as she couldn't leave her charges in varying stages of the disease. He came, but she refused to see him lest he might carry the infection back to Pasquelo.

August came and went and Pasquelo left for college. Grant was lonely and had to content himself with his work and his weekly visits with the Acostas. He went to the valley frequently with eggs and chickens and any delicacy he thought might please the sick. Margarita was the last to succumb and had been ill for two weeks before Grant knew it. He came immediately and in spite of the doctor's orders pushed past Esta to the sickroom. He was amazed at the change in Margarita's appearance. She was thin, and her eyes were sunken.

He bent over and caressed her face, but there was no recognition in the dark eyes raised to his.

"Why wasn't I told of this?" he demanded.

"Señor Bera, she made us promise not to let you know," Esta said.

"Where's the doctor? Why isn't he here?"

"Dr. Barrerra went to the hotel for some lunch. He'll be back soon." Esta's eyes were red from weeping.

"I'm going to get her to a hospital," Grant said and hurried to the hotel.

"How is Margarita?" Henrietta asked.

"I just got here, so I don't know. She looks terribly ill to me. Where is the doctor?"

"Over there."

Grant approached him and made his plea, but Dr. Barrerra wouldn't consent to Margarita's being moved.

"And who are you?" the doctor asked.

"I'm sorry I didn't introduce myself. I'm Grant Bera. Margarita and I were to have been married weeks ago. If I can't take her to a hospital, I'd like to bring a nurse in here."

"I think Esta and Señora Martinez are doing all anyone can do, but if you'd feel better with a nurse in charge, get one."

Grant dashed back to check on Margarita again, spoke of his errand to Esta, and hurried on. It was dark when he returned but he brought a nurse with him.

"Is there any change, Doctor?"

"No perceptible change. We should know by midnight. No," at Grant's look of concern, "I'm not leaving. Now let's get out and let Nurse Costello take over."

Henrietta had made periodic visits ever since Margarita's illness. Now, on hearing the doctor's verdict, she came prepared to stay the night and joined Grant and Frank on the small porch for the vigil. Dr. Barrerra remained in the sickroom. Grant consulted his watch frequently and at twelve o'clock returned to stand beside the bed. The doctor was bent over listening to Margarita's heartbeat.

"Well?" Grant asked as he stood erect.

"She's still breathing fitfully, but her heart seems stronger. Why don't you go home and get some sleep? You can't do anything by staying here."

In reply, Grant took the chair at the head of the bed. The nurse looked at the doctor who shook his head in a gesture of defeat.

"They were to have been married when this epidemic broke out," he explained.

Margarita's recovery was slow. Grant stayed in the valley until she improved to where he felt it safe to leave her, then returned two or three times a week. On each visit he urged an immediate marriage.

"Let's wait a little longer, Grant, until I'm feeling more like myself," she begged.

"Well, I won't insist until you're stronger, but I'm

tired of waiting. I suppose you had the same letter from Pasquelo that I had. I brought mine along in the event you wanted to read it."

"Of course I do!" She took the note and read.

Dear Dad,

I suppose you and Mother have both received the report on my grades. I'm ashamed of that math and I'm going to improve on it this month. I find it hard to study with all the noise and confusion we have, guys running in and out, transistor radios blaring. I wish I could get a room off campus. There isn't much chance of that, though. This is a college town and the students lucky enough to find space in private homes reserve them from year to year and then pass them on to relatives when they leave, so I'm told.

You'll never guess who's in my English class—a nephew of your friend Mr. Scott. He wants to see the pictures I took when we were on the tour. Will you please send them when you have time?

Roy has asked me to go home with him for supper tonight and to study for an exam tomorrow. He lives with a widowed aunt a little way out of town. He says it's so quiet out there you can hear a pin drop.

Guess I'd better attack the books. I want to devote the time tonight to studying for the test.

Pasquelo

"Did you think his grades were so bad?"

"They certainly weren't good, Margarita. Of course, it's going to take a while for him to adjust. All this is entirely new to him, but he'll make it."

"I still think it would have been better if he had stayed in Mexico for his education. Our schools here are as good as any across the border."

"I agree, but he had his heart set on this college—and he needs the chance to test his 'wings.' If he always had us to cushion his falls he'd never be able to stand the hard knocks life deals everyone. Who knows, after a year away he may want to come home to our own university. . . .Now I've got to be going. It seems all I ever do is say 'good-bye' to you. I hope we'll soon be changing that."

Chapter 24

"I don't believe I could have endured another day in that classroom," Isobel said to her brother as she dropped her purse on the couch and collapsed beside it.

"I feel the same way. I don't know why the work seems to get harder the nearer you get to the end of the term," John agreed.

"You haven't changed your mind about going to New York with me?"

"No, Bel, all I want right now is to rest—right here. I may make another tour of the ruins later on. When do you leave?"

"Next Wednesday. I doubt that I'd make the trip if it weren't for Mildred's marriage. But Edna, Kitty, and I promised Mildred that we'd be attendants at each other's wedding."

"Why would anyone name a girl after a cat? You never heard of anyone being called 'Puppy.' "

"Her name is Katherine Hawk. Somebody at Graceland began calling her 'Kitty Hawk,' and the nickname stuck. Now I think I'll shower and lie down until time for supper."

"We'll go out and eat after you've rested. Hand me the mail as you pass the desk, please."

Isobel complied and sat down again with her own letters.

"This is a coincidence. Here's an ad from a travel agency advertising a tour of the ruins in lower Mexico and Guatemala," John exclaimed.

"Why don't you go? I doubt that our old car could stand such a long trip."

"So do I. The tour leaves in just ten days. That doesn't give me much time to argue the point with myself, does it?"

"Go on, Johnny. I won't feel so guilty about leaving you if you do."

"I think you've just talked me in to it. Now . . . tell me your news."

"It's just girl-talk—plans for the wedding. I'm to stay with Kitty in New Jersey."

"You'll have a great time. And see as much of New York as you can so you can tell me all about it when you come home."

Chapter 25

Dear Dad,

When are you and Mother going to get married? I thought she would have moved to the ranch by this time. I want both of you there when I come home.

I told you I was going to study for a test with Roy Bond. The place where he lives is out of town—a big house set down in the middle of an Iowa cornfield. Mrs. McCoy, Roy's aunt, doesn't farm it; she has the land out on lease.

You'd like her, Dad. She's short and fat with round, red cheeks and the bluest eyes you ever saw. She's always smiling. Roy said her husband used to call her "Dumpling" because she was so chubby and the family shortened it to "Dump." I thought Roy was being rude when he called her "Aunt Dump" until he explained.

I almost forgot the most important piece of news. Mrs. McCoy is willing to let me stay here, too, if Roy and I can share a room. I plan to move as soon as I get clearance from the dean. I'll tell you all about it in my next letter.

Pasquelo

Grant read the letter again, then put it aside to take to Margarita. "I'm glad he's happy. I wish I could say the same for myself."

Dear Señor Faz,

Did you ever see it snow? I had my first experience with it this week. It began falling while we were in class—just big, soft isolated flakes at the start, but by the time we left for home the ground was covered. It was exciting to me, but Roy said it wouldn't be so thrilling if I had to dig a car out of the drifts before I could get it started. He may be right.

I like the place where I'm staying. I'm living in a private home. We're quite a household—two middle-aged women and three students, all boys. Both the ladies are nice, but I like Mrs. McCoy better. Miss Jessie is tall and thin, and suffering with what she calls 'my sinuses.' She sniffles constantly in spite of a mint scented cloth she holds to her nose. Mrs. McCoy is cheerful; Miss Jessie is full of apprehensions. She thinks that we don't have enough wood and coal to last us through the winter, that the house is going to catch fire and burn down, that the water pipes will burst from the cold, and that the vegetables will all freeze.

Roy is popping corn over the hearth fire and I want in on that, so I'll write more next time.

Pasquelo

Frank put the letter back in its envelope. He looked through the open window to his patio garden now in full bloom, glad that he didn't have to worry about frozen pipes or frosted flowers.

"I can't imagine anyone living in a place like that when he can have this," he told himself. "I suppose I have the soil of Mexico in my blood, for I love my country."

212

Outside the storm raged and a rush of wind sent the snow against the window panes. An occasional ping on the glass evidenced the presence of ice crystals.

Pasquelo parted the draperies and tried to see out, but everything was shrouded in the white mantle that encased the farmhouse. He readjusted the curtains and looked around the room with satisfaction. The flames in the hearth leaped up and retreated in rhythm with the wailing wind. A heap of glowing embers had been raked to the front of the fireplace and over these rested a Dutch oven from which a tantalizing odor escaped. All three of the boys turned frequently to inhale the spicy fragrance.

"Just about ten minutes more, boys," Miss Dump said, lifting the lid, "and the apples will be ready. Want to bring the bowls and spoons and a pitcher of cream? Oh—get the TV tables and set them up." Pasquelo and Kevin brought the tables from the closet under the stairway, while Roy got the items from the kitchen.

"Boy, it's cold out there!" Pasquelo said when they returned.

"I think you'd better get a sweater on, Pasquelo. We don't want you catching cold," Miss Dump said.

"Don't you ever have snow in Mexico?" Kevin asked.

"Not where I live. The mountains get it, of course; some of them are always snow covered, but my home is in the warmer part of the country. We think it's cold sometimes, but it's never like this." The boys arranged the tables and returned to their seats, Miss Dump to her knitting, and Miss Jessie to her crocheting—and sniffling. Pasquelo looked on for a moment, then took a sheet of paper and began to write.

Dear Mamá,

I believe Roy was right when he said it was so quiet out here you could hear a pin drop. The farm is a half mile from the highway, so the noise of passing traffic is lessened. We leave it all behind when we turn into the lane leading to the McCoy place. I pay half of Roy's car expenses for the ride to and from school.

It's snowing again, and the wind beats against the house as if it's trying to tear the place apart. The roof has a steep pitch to prevent an accumulation of snow which might cause damage if allowed to pile up. Our bedrooms are all upstairs so we hear the cadence of the wind and the rain and the sleet distinctly. It makes our beds seem cozier by contrast.

You said you wanted to know all the details of my new life. I like it here, and if I couldn't live in Mexico I believe I'd choose Iowa. I'm getting better grades than I did when I first came. One reason, I think, is because I've learned the routine. And it's easier for me to study now, for until we've finished our homework Mrs. McCoy says no radio or television.

You asked about our food. It's different from what we have at home, and frankly, I get hungry for tortillas. We have a lot of ham and bacon and eggs, and Miss Jessie makes biscuits; they're good. Mrs. McCoy raises pigs and chickens, so we have plenty of meat. And we have a snack every night after we've finished studying. Tonight we're having baked apples with cream. She says they're ready, and so am I.

Pasquelo

Dear Pasquelo,

There's nothing new here at the ranch. I went to church Sunday morning, then drove down to the valley to watch the local boys play the team from Delgado. Both groups were good, but Frank's won by several points.

I spent Saturday with your mother and stopped again Sunday evening to take her to the hotel for supper. We never have an opportunity to talk at her home. I don't know when she'll feel free to come here to stay. Lola is expecting a baby and has been quite ill—so ill that Joe has moved her back to your mother's and hired a woman to come in and take care of her during the day. Since Lola came home to be with her, Margarita can't leave now. If all goes well, however, we should be married in three or four months.

I miss the Acostas. With both of them gone I have no real close friends here. John thought his sister would be home by now and asked me to check on her occasionally and see if she needed anything. I went over yesterday; no one was there but the maid.

I'm glad that you've moved into a private home. This first year is a sharp break for you, and being in a new school in a foreign country could make adjusting difficult. I'm sure your next grades will show a marked improvement.

Dad

———————

Pasquelo had developed a chest cold and Aunt Dump had insisted that he stay home.

"But every day is so important," he'd argued.

"Not as much as your health. What would be the advantage of going out in the snow for a day's schooling and then landing in the hospital for a month with pneumonia?"

215

"I'm sure you're right, but I'm so weak in math; it has plagued me all the way through school."

"Get your books and I'll tutor you; I used to teach at Graceland, you know. On second thought, with your tendency to cough I don't think you should try to talk. Jessie will soon have that cough syrup ready; it should soothe your throat."

"If you'll tell me where it is I'll get it."

"Jessie's making it. It's a good remedy. I don't know what she puts in it for she has never let me watch her concoct it. She brought the formula when she came here."

"How long has she lived with you?"

"Oh, twenty-five or thirty years, I suppose. Jessie's a good woman—a thoroughly good person."

"Here you are, Pasquelo." Miss Jessie entered on the tail of Aunt Dump's eulogy. "It's still pretty warm, but not too warm. Take this spoonful. You should be getting some relief from that sore throat in an hour or so."

She administered the medication and then said, "This is good soup weather and we have an ailing boy on our hands. He shouldn't eat anything heavy as long as he has a fever. The old Dominick hen hasn't laid an egg in months, so I think I'll yank her head off and put her in the pot."

"Good planning, Jessie. Do you need some help?"

"Land, no! I'm going to hang the kettle over this fire and have it handy, as well as save the trouble of lighting one in the kitchen." Miss Jessie left the room and a moment later they heard the back door close as she went on her murderous mission.

"Jessie's had a hard and unrewarding life," Aunt Dump said.

As the observation didn't seem to require an answering comment, Pasquelo turned back to his books.

Miss Jessie had had a hard life. Orphaned in early childhood she had been passed from one relative to another until she had landed on the McCoy doorstep, all her earthly possessions in a cardboard suitcase and a shopping bag.

"I'm your cousin, Jessie Osgood, and I've come to visit you." She delivered her introductory speech just as her sister had drilled her carefully on it. "Just say you've come to visit," she had been told, "but stay as long as they'll have you. That's a college town where they live, so maybe you can get a job. And for goodness sake, Jessie, fix up a bit. Perhaps you can get a husband and won't be a burden on the family."

So poor Jessie's visit had extended over the years. There was scant opportunity for regular employment in Lamoni, but whenever extra hands were needed, Jessie's were requisitioned. Sometimes the service was paid for, more often not.

Aunt Dump and Pasquelo moved aside when she came in later with the iron kettle and adjusted it on the hook over the fire. After getting the coals situated under it she picked up her Bible and took her accustomed seat on the far side of the chimney. For a time they were all absorbed in their reading. Then

Miss Jessie suddenly lowered her book, and looking over the rim of her glasses said, "I wonder if anyone has ever painted a picture of God."

"Oh, yes, Jessie; some have had the audacity to try it."

"You'd think that people would have more respect for spiritual things, wouldn't you? I wonder how they ever got that way."

"It's been a gradual falling away. I sometimes think it wouldn't be a bad idea for the preachers to inspire a little fearful awe in us. The Bible is full of the loving regard in which the Hebrews held God—for example the nineteenth Psalm:

> The heavens declare the glory of God;
> and the firmament showeth his handiwork.
> Day unto day uttereth speech,
> and night unto night showeth knowledge.

And, of course, the Twenty-third Psalm:

> The Lord is my shepherd; I shall not want.
> ...Yea, though I walk through the valley
> of the shadow of death, I will fear no evil,
> for Thou art with me.

"Is that in the Bible?" Pasquelo asked.

"Yes, it is, Pasquelo. Would you like for me to recite all of it?"

"Would you, please?"

In reverent tones, she proceeded to repeat the lines that have comforted believers ever since a lonely man composed them for his own reassurance.

218

"Thank you, Aunt Dump. That's beautiful."

"I don't suppose many of us today subscribe to that. Those people back there acknowledged God's omnipotence, his righteousness, his love and his mercy." She paused for a moment, seeming to weigh the words for her next statement. "We've gotten so chummy with him that we seem to have forgotten the magnitude of his being."

"I never thought of that!" Pasquelo said.

"Few of us do. And I think one reason that we've gotten so far from regarding him as a Father is because children have ceased to respect their earthly parents. Dad has become the butt of jokes in every level of society. Among the ancients he was the last word in authority. He had the power of life and death over his family. Today he's often made to look incompetent. Perhaps that's the reason we've become careless with God."

"Well, I don't consider Dad stupid . . . nor my father, either," Pasquelo declared.

"Is the person you call 'Dad' your grandfather?" Miss Jessie asked.

"No, Dad is my best friend, but no relation. He's paying for my education. Papá died when I was ten, and if it hadn't been for Dad I would have had to quit school after the sixth grade."

"He must be a good man."

"He is, and my father was the greatest."

"It's refreshing to see a young man with your attitude." Miss Jessie arose to add more water to the soup kettle.

"Mrs. McCoy, how do you know there is a God? Not that I doubt his existence, but I never saw anyone so absolutely sure of it as you are." Kevin had come in silently. "You've never seen him."

"How do I know that God exists? Kevin, I can say with Job, 'I know that my Redeemer lives,' but before I had that surety I had faith, and my faith grew to become knowledge."

"But what if you don't have faith?"

"All of us have faith. If we didn't we couldn't get through a single day. If you didn't have faith that your car would start in the morning you wouldn't get out of bed at six o'clock in the morning. You don't know that its mechanical parts will be in running order until you try it. So it is with God. He has told us to prove him. He invites testing. We have no excuse, Kevin, for not knowing beyond the shadow of a doubt that he lives. As for my having seen a visible form...no, I haven't...but I have felt his presence many times, and I have every evidence of his being. I have seen his artistry in the morning and evening sky. I have heard his voice in the song of birds and the murmur of a stream. I have witnessed his power in the roaring surf and in a winter's storm. I have felt his serenity in the falling snow and a gentle spring rain. I have seen his majesty in the mountains, his grandeur in the flash of lightning. I have known the mercy of his healing touch and his compassion in taking a sufferer home. I have seen his love expressed in the eyes of a mother and felt it in the embrace of a loved one. This may have no meaning yet for you, Kevin, but it does for me. I *know* that my Father lives."

"Mrs. McCoy, you're a poet! Neither Shelly nor Keats could improve that! As I said at first, I have never doubted the existence of a Supreme Creator. I used to think your church was queer but now that I've heard you explain it I see that you have many beliefs in common with other churches. I've discussed your faith with my grandmother—rather critically, at times, I'll admit. She advised me not to jump to conclusions, and to quote her, 'The joker in the deck may be you. It's possible that you're the odd-ball.' "

"My brother-in-law once told my sister about the same thing. He said, 'Never toss a rock at a strange hat. Some day you may be under it,' " Miss Jessie offered her bit.

As a hissing sound came from the pot Miss Jessie leaped to her feet, grabbed the teakettle, and poured more water into the soup. "I got so interested in the conversation that I forgot about our supper," she said. "Now I hate to leave but I must go down to the cellar and get the vegetables for the soup. Then the cow must be milked."

"Jessie, I'll finish the soup. You go on with your chores. Darkness comes early, and it'll turn colder toward night."

Chapter 26

"It's going to seem mighty quiet around here without Lola and the baby." Esta was busy setting the house in order after Joe had taken his family home.

"Yes, it will be different after the hectic last few months. But I'm so glad that it's over and that the baby and Lola are all right. I look forward to relaxing for a while."

"With the strain you've been under you'd better make it a long while!"

"I can't pamper myself—there's too much sewing piled up. I'll have a cup of coffee then start on one of the dresses I have cut out."

Soon both women were absorbed in their work.

When shadows began to lengthen Margarita said, "There, I'm glad it's time to quit. It's been a profitable day.... I hope we can do as well tomorrow." She arose and pushed the machine against the wall. "Did anyone get the mail?"

"I didn't see it. Rosa, did you go to the post office?"

"Si, here are your letters and the newspaper."

"Here's one from my boy," Margarita said as she tore the envelope open eagerly and read its contents. This was soon accomplished for the letter was short. Esta could tell that she was disappointed and a little disturbed. "He wants me to consent to his joining that church," she said. "I don't know what to say."

"I think it's wonderful," Esta said.

"You would! It seems that Pasquelo has grown completely away from me," she continued. "We have nothing in common anymore. He used to be so interested in the affairs of the village; now he never mentions his old friends."

"Well, he's young, and he's made a lot of new friends. With his studies and sports and social life he must be very busy."

"No, Esta, all this began before he left the valley. He began turning from me to Grant a long time ago."

"Isn't it normal for a boy to want male companionship?"

"Yes," Margarita sighed, "I suppose it is."

"Well, all this will straighten out when you marry Señor Bera. Isn't that a letter from him?"

"Yes. I wonder why he's writing now. He will be here Saturday." Margarita opened the single sheet of paper and scanned it quickly. "That impatient man! Do you know he wants to get married next Sunday? He says he saw Joe in the City and learned that he was taking Lola and little Joe home today, and he reminds me that I promised we'd be married as soon as they left.

"Are you going through with it, Mamá?"

"I'd rather not. . . . I'm not prepared. But I suppose I will since I promised."

"You don't want to marry him?" Esta asked in surprise.

"Of course I want to marry him, but not in such a

hurry. I'll call him tomorrow and try to reason with him."

The household settled down early. It would be the first night of undisturbed rest for some time, and Margarita and Esta sank onto their beds gratefully. Some time later they were aroused by the clatter of running feet over the cobblestones, then the furious pounding on Frank's door, and his response.

"Tell Henrietta not to worry. I'll be up immediately."

Margarita opened her door and looked out. "What's wrong, Frank?"

"Henry's violently ill and Henrietta wants to get him into Cuernavaca at once. I've got to drive around and get on the highway so I can get the car to the hotel entrance."

"I'd better dress and go up there," Margarita decided.

"Good! Tell Henrietta I'll be there as fast as I can make it."

When Margarita got there Henrietta was hovering over the bed trying to reassure Henry as well as herself that all would be well.

"I can't think what can be wrong. He's never been sick since we married," she told Margarita.

"Frank will be here in a minute, Henrietta. Change your clothes. You can't go to the hospital in your gown. Where are Henry's clothes? I'll pack a few changes of pajamas for him."

"You'll go in with us, won't you, Margarita?"

"Of course. Here, you're not matching buttons and buttonholes. And where is your belt?"

"I don't know and it doesn't matter." Henrietta ran back to the bed where Henry was trying to stifle his groans.

Frank had padded the back of the station wagon with blankets, and he and Henrietta helped Henry down the hotel steps and onto the improvised bed. Dr. Barrerra met them at the hospital and after a hurried examination rushed the patient to the operating room.

Margarita and Frank stayed until dawn. Henry was in his own room, and Henrietta sat with him until a nurse came in to take over.

"I know you have to get back to the valley," she told her friends. "Margarita, is it too much to ask you to take charge of the hotel until I can leave here?"

"You know I will, Henrietta," was Margarita's prompt reply.

"And I'll spend as much time there as I can. Between the two of us maybe business won't suffer too much," Frank added. "If we leave now, we'll just about make it in time for school."

"Please, I *must* have some coffee first," Margarita implored.

"Oh, we'll take time for a quick breakfast. There's a restaurant around the corner. I patronized it last night," and Frank turned the car in that direction.

"Grant isn't going to be pleased with this," Margarita said as they were seated.

"He surely won't object to your sharing a meal with me!" Frank exclaimed.

"I didn't mean that. I was referring to my having to take over the hotel management while Henry's in the hospital. You see, he's coming Saturday expecting to be married. It's just impossible—I can't let those two down after all they've done for me."

"That *is* bad, but he'll understand."

"I wonder how long I'll be needed."

"I heard the doctor tell Henrietta that, barring complications, Henry should be back on his feet in about three weeks."

"Well, I'll stay on if it takes twice that long."

The waiter brought their coffee, then the food, and a half hour later they were on their way to the valley.

Once at home Margarita explained the situation to Esta as she got into a uniform. "It's going to be hard on you, Esta, but it's unavoidable."

"The girls and I will manage."

Saturday came and so did Grant.

"I won't deny that I'm terribly disappointed, Margarita. All my plans are made, even to our wedding supper. I wouldn't ask you to desert your friends, but I've waited so long!" he said.

"I'm disappointed, too, Grant, but I couldn't say 'no' when Henrietta asked me. On your way back, why don't you stop at the hospital and ask how Henry is."

"I surely will. I'll see him if it's possible."

So Grant left Margarita standing on the hotel steps.

She watched after him until business called her inside again.

It was a month before the doctor would dismiss Henry. Frank went in to Cuernavaca and brought him home. Margarita had a hammock set up on the patio, feeling sure he would want to be where the activity was, even though he couldn't participate. She refused to leave her post until Henrietta had had a few days rest. At the end of that time she was glad to go home.

"I'm going to bed, Esta, and I don't want to stir for a week," she declared.

"You do that. I'll try to keep the noise down while you sleep."

Two days later Margarita again took command of the household. She was at the hotel when Grant came the following weekend. He spent a few minutes with Henry, stopped to speak to Henrietta, then took Margarita's arm and urged her toward home.

"It's time I took charge of you," he said. "You're absolutely wasting away."

"I have lost some weight," she confessed, "and I doubt that I'll ever feel really rested again."

"You will after you've been at the ranch for a while. Are you ready to go back with me?"

"Oh, Grant! I can't possibly!"

"Why?"

"A lot of things. I don't think I should leave Henrietta yet. And Esta needs to be relieved of some responsibility for a while. She'll have it all when I'm gone. And since I've gotten thinner none of my clothes fit; I need to make some new ones."

"I'll take you into Mexico City and you can buy what you want already made."

"I prefer making my own clothes!" she said firmly.

He stopped and turned her to face him. "Margarita, you've been delaying our wedding for one reason or another for months! I'm tired of waiting, and I'm beginning to wonder if you really want to marry me!" His voice was firm, too.

"Perhaps I don't! Maybe that's why I've been delaying the wedding! You say you're tired of waiting. I'm just as tired of being pushed. Here, take your ring and give it to someone who's eager to get married!"

"I'm sorry I spoke as I did, Margarita. You're not feeling well. Put the ring back on your finger, and let's go to the house where we can talk this over calmly."

"I'm perfectly well, and there's no need to argue the point. Now take the ring." He dropped it in his pocket and turned to leave. "And don't come back with it next weekend!" she called after him.

"Don't worry," he said, and strode off angrily. Margarita ran home crying.

"What's the matter, Mamá?" Esta followed her into the house, where she leaned against the door frame and let her tears fall. "You must tell me what's wrong!"

"You wouldn't understand."

"Try me and see."

"Esta, I'm not going to marry Grant."

"You're not? Why?"

"Because I can't stand his impatience and his

228

demanding ways. I've lived alone too long to start jumping when he speaks."

"I never thought of him as being that way. To me he seems gentle and easy-going."

"He was irritated because I wouldn't go back with him today...with no time to plan or get my clothes ready!"

"Well, I think he's been *very* patient. Just think of the many times you've put him off. I don't think many men would have had so much forbearance."

"And he came between Pasquelo and me. I always had a dutiful son until he went to Mexico City. At first he came home every time he had a chance, then his visits grew more and more infrequent....I hardly ever saw him. And I know he encouraged Pasquelo to go to that school in Iowa. He thought by getting him that far from me he would complete the break!"

"Now, Mamá, you know you don't believe that! Mr. Bera didn't cause the break if there was one. Time and circumstances bring changes to every family. When we're children home and family are our world. As we grow older our horizon widens. We find other interests and other friends. For Pasquelo there were school functions, clubs, sports. Until he moved from our village his vision was limited by the hills that surround the valley. Perhaps being introduced suddenly to city life brought the change sooner than you were ready to accept it. You're tired now. Put this out of your mind for a few days. Then after you're rested, think it over and write Señor Bera. He'll understand, I'm sure."

"Me apologize? Never!"

Chapter 27

Dear Mamá,

I wish you could have been here for my baptismal service. It was an experience I'll never forget. I've been studying the Bible and Book of Mormon a lot ever since, and this has been the most interesting evening I've ever spent. Some time ago I wrote you that Aunt Dump was teaching us from the Book of Mormon and I promised to share with you what I learned.

Tonight, after we'd finished our lesson, Miss Jessie turned on the TV. We got in on the middle of a protest meeting of college students. I never did learn what they were protesting, but the leader shouted 'God is dead!' and the whole group echoed his words. Then the camera was focused on a blonde who was absolutely beautiful until she joined in the yelling. You never saw such a change of expression. She suddenly became almost hideous. Miss Jessie turned the program off and Aunt Dump reached for her Book of Mormon and read, "They shall teach with their learning, and deny the Holy Ghost that gives utterance. And they deny the power of God; and they say to the people, 'Hearken to us, and hear our precept; for behold, there is no God today, for the Lord has done his work, and he has given his power unto men.' "

Isn't that remarkable? I had been seeing the fulfillment of prophecy made over two thousand years ago. It proves that at one time our forefathers were intrusted with the message this wonderful book bears.

Kevin has just come in and he's soaking wet. I'm glad we're getting some much needed rain tonight, but thunder and the lightning still startle me.

I'll have to stop writing now. Aunt Dump is afraid the lightning may hit our power line.

Keep studying the Book.

Pasquelo

Margarita read the letter aloud, then turned to stare through the door. "It seems that every letter I get from Pasquelo widens the gap between us. He's so absorbed in that book and in his church that he can talk of little else. And I can't even get interested."

"I can understand his enthusiasm, for it affected me the same way. When you've belonged to another church and the truth of this one is suddenly revealed to you it's as though a burst of light floods your mind. And then when you begin to understand the doctrine of the church and learn of its goals, it's like walking from night into day. But I can't explain it adequately—you have to experience it for yourself to understand how it touches Pasquelo," Esta said.

"Then I'm afraid I'll never understand," Margarita replied sadly.

Dear Mamá,

Many thanks for the "box of goodies," as Aunt Dump called it. I had some help emptying it, and all of us enjoyed it. I hope the orange trees continue to bear. The fruit isn't much, but the candied peel is terrific.

I've been thinking of home all day. I dreamed last night that I

231

was a kid again, working in my first garden. I suppose that's what got me to thinking and remembering things that happened then. Papá helped me sow the seeds. I had a row of onions, one of radishes, two tomato bushes, and a pepper plant. After they began bearing, every time we had vegetables on the table you told me they came from my garden.

I couldn't have been more than five when Papá bought Boliver for me. He called us his two colts.

Do you remember the costume you made for me to wear to the fiesta? It was of soft, shiny cloth. The pants were green, the shirt yellow, and I had a red hat to go with them. When I donned that outfit I thought I was really something.

Kids in this country don't know what they're missing, not having fiestas. Of course they have amusements that we don't have, but I've not seen anything that I think can compare with our village celebrations. For instance, the dimly lit plaza at night, the tantalizing odors rising from pots of chili, tamales, and coffee over braziers glowing with coals; men and boys harmonizing with the low strumming of guitars around the fountain. How I love my Mexico! We need never be ashamed of our nationality for we belong to the family of God's chosen, and he has made wonderful promises to us that will one day be fulfilled.

Pasquelo

P.S.

I've just read the above. I wrote it last night, but before I could finish the letter the fellows came down and wanted me to go into town with them to see a show. It was too late to write more when we returned so I'm at it again tonight.

I'm glad you're reading the Book of Mormon. If you approach it with an open mind you'll be convinced of its truth. I hope someday that you and Dad see this as I do and we can become a united family in the church.

232

P.S. again

I'm sure you've guessed from reading this that I was a little homesick last night. I was ready to chuck everything and take the first plane to Mexico. Luckily the fellows came in when they did. I feel much better now, but I've decided to finish my schooling at the university in Mexico City.

"Now that sounds like my boy," Margarita said with satisfaction when she had finished reading the letter. "I'll answer it immediately....I may not have time later on." She took pen and paper to the kitchen, put them on the table, and began to write:

My Dear Son,

Well, change has come to Alhaja at last. For some reason Father Felipe was transferred to another parish, and we have a new priest—quite a young man. Father Martiné Perieda is his predecessor's opposite. After mass the first morning he was here he put aside his clerical garb, donned khaki trousers, and worked in his garden until noon. When the team gathered for practice after school he joined the boys for a game. He is such a vibrant person...we never know where we'll find him or what he'll be doing. The children and young people love him, and I'll wager he'll have most of them attending church regularly before the year is out. He has fit into village life wonderfully well. Of course there are some of the older ones who can't reconcile his very human activities with his priestly calling. He has visited us several times, and although he knows that neither Esta nor I are members of his congregation he treats us as if we were the whitest of his sheep. He often shares a meal with the boys.

He wants to expand El Abrigo's kitchen and dining area to accommodate all the poorer children in school. He says children can't be expected to learn anything when they're hungry, and of course, he's right. It has been decided that we're to try it. Frank called a meeting of the sponsors, and after a lot of discussion the majority voted to follow Father Martiné's suggestion. I hope it works out satisfactorily. So much for village news.

Lechera has given us a calf—a little heifer. I don't know whether or not to sell her. Frank thinks we should keep her. He says we'll need more milk as we get more children.

The village boys won a game from the San Fernando team. From all the shouting they did I surmise it was quite a victory. Anselmo has developed into a very good ball player. They call him the Home Run King. He's very dear to me, and I'm proud of him and the way he has made a place not only in the Home but in the village as well.

We are all looking forward to seeing you. Esta and the boys send best wishes.

Love from Mamá

Dear Dad,

How are things at the ranch? I'm eager to get back to Mexico. I'm glad that the school year is nearly over and that my next will be spent at our own university.

I've been feeling pretty low the past few days. We've been discussing the Book of Mormon, as usual, and Aunt Dump read some of the prophecies concerning this "choice land."

I have always thought, as I believe most people have, that the United States was invincible. Aunt Dump says that the same conditions which caused the downfall of the mighty civilizations that once occupied these continents exist today and that our time is running out. She cites the rise in crime of all kinds, the spread of immorality, the loss of respect for God, even denial of his existence. And one great worry of hers is the increase of power in the subversive groups. She refers to the Book of Mormon where the people of that era were warned about letting such factions get a foothold. It plainly teaches that any country that shall uphold such secret associations and permit them to infiltrate society will be destroyed. The command is given that the government must be aroused to the danger and correct it, for if these groups are allowed to grow unchecked they will destroy the freedom of the entire world. It frightens me to think about it, for if this country is ever overcome the whole civilized world may well collapse. I wonder what it will take to alert our countries to the danger we're in.

Well, Dad, guess I'd better turn in and get some sleep. We get up at six o'clock, and it seems that I barely shut my eyes when the alarm rings. When I get home I'm going to sleep until noon every day for a month.

Pasquelo

Grant reread the letter, then turned to look out over the garden. "The quiet of this place has been getting on my nerves for a long time. As long as I had hope of Margarita's coming home I could stand it, but now I find it unbearable. I've got to do something about it. Now that the school year is over I think I'll see if one of the boys at Alhaja is interested in higher education. He can spend the summer with me and be ready for classes when the fall term begins."

So, after delivering eggs to the hotel in Mexico City, he drove on to the valley and stopped in front of the hotel. Henrietta rushed to meet him.

"Have you come for Margarita?" she whispered.

"No, I wish I had. I wonder if you'd let one of your

boys run down and tell Frank I'd like to meet him here? It's better for me to stay out of that end of the village."

"Sure, Domilito can go," and Henrietta sent the boy on the errand. When she was called into the kitchen Grant walked down to the fountain to wait for Frank.

"Sorry to bother you, Frank," he said, "but Margarita prefers that I keep my distance."

"No trouble at all. What's on your mind?"

"Frank, I'm lonely. I miss the boy noise more and more since both my youngsters left. I figure the only remedy for that is another boy. Do you have one ready to leave the shelter?"

"If I was a praying man, Grant, I'd say you were an answer to my petitions. Margarita and I have been racking our brains trying to think of some way to send Anselmo to school in Cuernavaca."

"Would you discuss this with her? If she approves I'd like to take the boy back with me, for I doubt that I'll be down this way again."

"I think she'll be more than willing. She's eager to place these youngsters where they can have maximum advantages."

"Well, if you'll approach Margarita about it I'll wait here for her answer."

"I know what it will be, Grant, but I'll talk it over with her."

Frank hurried on, eager to tell his news. "Margarita, what do you suppose has happened?"

"I have no idea."

"Grant wants another boy."

236

"How do you know?"

"He just told me. He's waiting in the village for your decision."

"That's wonderful! It's just the place for Anselmo. Let me call him."

But when the plan was laid before him he hesitated. "You won't be there, will you, Mamá?"

"No, Anselmo. This is my home."

"What about Bito? I'd like to go on to school, but I can't leave him. You know how the kids pick on him when I'm not around."

"I won't insist on it, Anselmo, if you don't want to go." Then to Frank she said, "I can't separate them. Neither would be happy if they were apart."

"And there's no other boy ready?"

"Not now. Perhaps later."

"I see. Well, I'll go tell Grant." So he returned and reported the result of his mission.

"Let both boys come. I can house a dozen. I usually have at least two on the place anyway. Tell her to pack them both up and send them to me. I'll wait for you here."

Frank returned promptly. "She's very pleased and very grateful," he said. "The boys will be along as soon as their clothes are put together. I told her we'd wait at the hotel." Grant arose from his seat on the rim of the fountain and they walked on slowly.

"Have you seen John lately?" Frank asked.

"Yes, night before last. We have supper together twice a week. He spends the rest of his time holding meetings in any home opened to him. And of course he has services at his church every Sunday."

"Poor old John! He was pretty sharp until he got carried away with religion. He's really a fanatic about the Book of Mormon...and the reason Isobel won't marry me is because I don't accept it."

"Why don't you?"

"Grant, I could probably take everything except how Joseph Smith came to write it."

"You mean you let that prejudice you against everything the book contains? So far as I can see its teachings correspond to those of the Bible."

"Well...that's something else I can't understand. Since it repeats biblical canons, why is it needed?"

"Frank, you're fulfilling the book's prophecy when you question that need—or so John told me. He quotes from the book in reference to the present day when it predicts that men shall say, 'We have received the word of God and don't need any more'...or words to that effect. He says because God spoke once doesn't mean that he can't and doesn't continue to speak. Your greatest objection is really modern revelation, isn't it?"

"That's part of it. Say, since you seem so conversant with the church beliefs, why haven't you been converted?"

"Perhaps I have, but I haven't joined yet."

"Why?"

"The standards are too high. I don't think I could live up to them. It's funny; the things you object to are the ones that appeal to me the most."

"How is that?"

"The Book of Mormon definitely establishes the

justice and mercy of God to all people, everywhere, and in every age. According to it God gave his laws to all men and they were commanded to write them so the people could be judged by them. How could a nation or a people be judged by laws they didn't know existed?"

"According to that there would be Scriptures of all kind floating around."

"I don't know about that but I can't believe that the Bible is the only account of God's word. Remember the Dead Sea Scrolls? Who knows what other records may be discovered?"

"Just do away with Joseph Smith's claim to divine revelation and I might be able to swallow the rest," Frank argued.

"People are converted to the church, Frank, not to Joseph Smith."

They reached the hotel, mounted the steps to the door, and paused there. The dining room was crowded.

"Looks as if Henry has a full house," Frank observed. "Let's go through the side entrance to the patio, there, to the left of the shrine." They retraced their steps and paused before the cross-crowned chapel. A statue of the sorrowing Virgin stood in an embankment of flowers; two tall candles cast a dim glow throughout the small recess.

"I never noticed that before. Does the hotel maintain it?" Grant asked.

"Oh, yes. Fresh candles and flowers are placed there every morning."

'I didn't know the Hernandez were that devout."

"Well, I'm not sure if it's religion or good business. They are Protestants...so draw your own conclusions," Frank explained wryly. "Sit there in the summer house while I get us some coffee."

They hadn't waited long when the boys came. Anselmo carried both bags of clothes.

"I'll bet they'd like a dish of ice cream, Frank," Grant said as Bito crowded onto the same chair with Anselmo.

"The hotel doesn't serve ice cream, but I can get them frescos. How about it, fellows?"

"Oh, yes, we'd like that very much! Red ones, please."

Frank filled the cones and brought them out. "Here, Bito, suppose you take this other chair. That will give you both more room." Bito moved over, and the boys happily consumed their refreshments while Grant finished his coffee.

"Thank you, Señor," Anselmo said. "I almost forgot."

"Thank you, Señor," Bito parroted. "I almost forgot."

"You're very welcome, boys. Now let's go." Grant stopped at the door to wave good-bye to the Hernandez, then led the boys to his car and drove off. Frank looked after them for a moment, then went inside to help out at the counter during the rush hour.

Chapter 28

"Manuela, where are the boys?" Grant asked the next morning.

"They're working in the garden."

"Did you send them?"

"No, Señor, Anselmo said his mama told them they were to make themselves useful," the cook replied.

"Well, I certainly didn't expect them to start as soon as they got here. I'll go see how they're getting along." From the patio Grant could see Anselmo diligently hoeing, but Bito wasn't in sight. He strolled down and discovered the small boy all but hidden by the plants he was weeding.

"I wish we had a papá like other kids," Bito was saying. "Why don't we?"

"Oh, some kids are just lucky. But we've got it real good at that. We have a nice place to stay—even better than Abrigo—plenty to eat, and this fall we'll go to a big school. I remember what it was like before I went to the shelter. I was always hungry in the daytime and cold at night."

Grant had heard enough. He turned and strode off to the chicken runs. He returned a moment later and announced his presence by stumbling against a post.

"Good morning, Señor."

"Good morning, boys. There's the breakfast bell so

let's not keep Manuela waiting. How would you like
to drive into town with me to deliver eggs to the
hospital? Have you seen the market?"

"No, Señor, we've never been here except that time
at Christmas."

"All right, run in and wash up. We'll leave in about
an hour."

They dropped their hoes and started a race to the
house; then, remembering their tools, they went back
and put them away. Grant gave them a nod of
approval when they passed him again.

"Bito, give me your plate so I can serve you." Grant
took the dish and began filling it.

"More squash, please, Señor. I like a lot of squash,"
Bito said.

"Eat what's on your plate, Bito, and if you want
more you may have it. Manuela prepares enough food
to feed the Mexican army. Anselmo, may I have your
plate?"

"I like squash, too, Señor, and corn—with lots of
butter on it."

"I've noticed that." Grant filled the plate.

They ate in silence for a while, then Grant put his
knife and fork down and leaned across the table.

"Boys," he began, "I think we're too formal around
here. I don't like your addressing me as 'señor.' I'd
much rather you'd call me papá. All the boys who have
stayed here did, and I'd rather be papá than 'señor.'"

Grant smiled. It was good to have a family again.

242

Chapter 29

John told his fellow tourists good-bye in Mexico City and hurried home to exchange experiences with Isobel. But instead of his sister, he was greeted by her letters. They were numbered in sequence of their writing, so he selected the first and began reading.

Dear Johnnie,

I am keeping my promise to write you as soon as I arrived, even though you're on your tour and won't read this until your return.

Edna has a small apartment which she shares with another teacher. It's terribly crowded—no patio, no yard or garden, not even a window box. I miss the spaciousness of our little home. I'll be here only until after the wedding on Friday, then I'll go to Trenton, New Jersey, with Kitty.

It's wonderful being with the girls again. We sat up most of last night talking, recalling college days.

There really isn't much to write about yet. I'm going to take the ferry around the Island tomorrow, then go to the top of the Empire State Building. The girls are still busy with their classes so I'll have to join a tour or go alone. I'll tell you about it later.

All my love,

Bel

Succeeding letters told of places she had visited and people she had met. She seemed to be enjoying a lot of activities, and he was glad. Perhaps it would take her mind off Frank. But he hurried on to her last letter, eager to learn when she would be home. The message left him numb.

I know this will come as a shock to you, and I'm not yet used to the idea myself. I have decided to stay here in New Jersey and work as a Spanish tutor. I had no idea of doing this when I left or I would have told you. Kitty has persuaded me to try it for a while. This separation may be good for both of us. We had begun to depend on each other far too much. Perhaps my being away may inspire you to seek other feminine society. I hope so.

John put the letter aside and thought about his sister's comment. Then he picked it up again and read on.

Please have Daisy pack the rest of my clothes and ship them to me.

She was really serious. . . . This little sister of his was striking out on her own.

When he saw the trunk being loaded the next day, John felt that he was closing a door on a part of his life.

Without Isobel sitting opposite him at the table he got the car out and drove over to the ranch.

"Come in, John, and tell me about your trip," was Grant's welcome. "Is the car operating as it should? I went over a few times and took it out on the road—enough to keep it in tune, I hope."

"It runs fine, Grant. I appreciate your keeping an eye on the place while I was away."

"Glad to do it. I went over at least once a week to see if Isobel needed anything, but she hadn't gotten home."

"No. . . well. . . Isobel isn't coming home. She's going to teach in New Jersey."

"Why would she decide to do that?"

"She thinks we both need a change and this is one way to effect it."

"I'm sorry, John."

"So am I. In fact, I'm lost without her. How does a man adjust to such a situation?"

"We learn, believe me. It isn't easy, but we learn. Say, I was just sitting down to supper. Why don't you join me and tell me about your trip?"

"There were thirty in the group. Some weren't careful about what they ate and drank, so we were delayed a couple of days while they recuperated. But I don't think anyone minded—I know I didn't. The hotel where we stayed was pleasant and the proprietors were friendly. It was a perfect place to rest. We climbed the mountain behind the village during the day, and at night someone always appeared with a guitar and we joined in singing.

"We had an amusing experience the first evening we were there—at least four of us men did. We were all billeted in one room—Earle Goodman, Gordon Williams, Tom Trundle, and I. We were eager to get under the shower, but were going through that 'you go first' routine when Earle hit upon the plan of using the bathroom alphabetically. You can't precede A so I got the first bath and Gordon was last. He crowed over the rest of us because, he said, being the last he could linger as long as he liked. He went in whistling and we could hear the splash of running water, then silence. Suddenly there was a veritable explosion and out came Gordon, lathered from head to toe. 'What's the matter with this place?' he yelled. 'The water's stopped running. Did you guys pull a fast one on me?' I went downstairs to investigate and found that water for the bathrooms was carried from a well on the plaza to a reservoir on the roof where the sun could warm it. We were not expected, so the hotel managers weren't prepared for so many all at once. As soon as they knew the storage tank was empty they had it filled."

"What did the chap with all the soap on him do?" Grant asked.

"He wiped off as much as he could and waited until we got the signal that all was well on the roof."

"Was he angry?"

"No, he treated it as a joke...said it was something to tell the folks back home."

"Did all the members of your group speak Spanish?"

"No, none of them did except a scholarly gentleman whom I learned was dean of romance languages at the University of New York. He was quite fluent most of the time. The dialects sometimes stumped him, so I served as interpreter—especially when ordering food or drinks and when shopping in the markets."

"Must be interesting to be a tour director."

"Not for me," John said quickly. "My roots are too deep to permit my wandering all over the country.It's no job for a man who loves his home. I doubt that I

246

would have gone on the tour if I'd known Isobel wasn't here to look after things."

"Come over often, John. I'm always here now—even on weekends."

"I'll remember that, Grant, and you come over when you can."

Chapter 30

My Dear Son,

You should have been home last week. I believe we held the largest fiesta we have ever had. You remember Henrietta's little placard in the hotel explaining El Abrigo? Well, some of the tourists have come down from time to time to look us over, and many of them have left generous contributions. Several months ago a lady in one of the groups became quite interested in us and asked all sorts of questions. When she went home she gave a talk on the tour before her club. She collected a hundred dollars (U.S. money) for the shelter. In some way the governor of her state heard of this and wanted to see for himself how we operate. He was commissioned to bring the money to us. Of course, there was a lot of correspondence concerning his trip. He wanted to see a real Mexican fiesta and planned his visit to coincide with one of ours. The news that our governor was bringing another from the north to Alhaja spread like fire, and people began gathering several days ahead of the event. Since they thought El Abrigo would be the main attraction they set their booths up all around us and the schoolhouse. Remundo was kind enough to let Joe spend the entire week in our end of the valley to insure protection and privacy.

I was with this Governor Cassels an entire afternoon. He found some of our ways interesting, some amusing. He couldn't get over Ignacio and Willie playing checkers on the park bench day after day. I told him that they were as much a part of the scenery as the bandstand. He thought Cabezo riding into the village on the tailend of his donkey "very picturesque" and couldn't see what kept him from sliding off. The market fascinated him, and Frank, who was his guide on that tour, said he would have sampled food from every pot if he hadn't been advised against it.

He was a delightful guest of the village because he was so enthusiastic about everything. When he left he gave Frank the money the ladies had sent and added a like amount from his own pocket. That means new clothes for all the boys as well as some much needed furnishings for the shelter. We took advantage of the wide selection of items we had during the week and replenished our supplies of both food and household goods.

Do you remember Señora Casavegas who used to come from Toluca with handwoven serapes and straw mats? She was here again after an absence of several years. The boys all needed new blankets for their beds so I let them choose their own. And I almost forgot...Bill Travieso asked to be remembered to you. He's living in Cuatla now and brought a load of sandals and woven net bags. I bought sandals for everyone and some of the bags; they will be ideal for holding beans and seed corn.

It was an exciting week and a very productive one for Alhaja, but I'm glad it's over and we can settle down to the peace and quiet of our valley. For the first time since the fiesta began Esta and I sat on the patio after supper enjoying the serenity of the night. We watched the cars and trucks climb the mountain behind the hotel and if we hadn't known differently we'd have mistaken their taillights for those of airplanes. The mountains don't look so high in daylight, but in the dusk they seem to reach into the sky.

Well, Estancio has just stuck his head out the door to remind us that it's time for the boys' nightcap of hot chocolate, so I must close.

I am counting the days until your return.

Love from Mamá

It was near sunset and the village noises had muted to a murmur as families gathered for the evening meal. From her seat beneath the poinciana tree which shed its blossoms and their glow over her, Margarita watched the boys take their places at the supper table. She smiled fondly as they bowed their heads while Father Martiné blessed their food.

"Won't you have supper with us, Father?" Esta asked.

"Thank you, Esta. Another time, perhaps. Joe is waiting to take me to see Justo Jiminez. His horse kicked him in the head and Joe thinks I should see him right away. But from the looks of that table you have a wonderful meal, so enjoy it with thanksgiving." And the priest was gone.

Margarita opened the book on her lap as Frank crossed the yard and took the chair opposite.

"I see you're reading it, too," he said.

"Studying it," she corrected.

"You're right, it demands study. Is it any less puzzling than it was?"

"Yes, I believe I'm gaining a better understanding. I've learned that it has none of the offensive teachings some people attribute to it. Its instructions are as uplifting and demanding as those of the Bible, and its prophets just as vigorous in condemning evil," Margarita said.

"That has been my experience, too. And I find that many of my objections are being eliminated one by one. At first I rejected the claim that the Americans were colonized in part by Israelites. Then the study of some of the sacred books of the early peoples, as well as the conclusions of some of our scientists, erased my doubts. I ridiculed the idea that Christ had ever visited these American continents; I now believe that it's entirely possible. But present-day revelation. . .I do have difficulty accepting as fact the tale of the golden plates being found in a hillside and translated by a farm boy."

The scramble from the table interrupted their conversation.

"Have supper with us tonight, Frank?" Margarita asked. "The girls will soon have the table cleared and reset."

"Thank you, I will. But I'd better tell Esta not to prepare for me at home. Esta," he called, "I'm joining you ladies tonight, so please set a place for me."

"I have already!"

Margarita and Frank took seats at the table and Esta whispered a simple grace.

"In a recent letter Pasquelo commented on the political situation in the world," Margarita said, as they began their meal. "He's deeply troubled over the future of the United States. He feels that the country isn't living up to its obligations and spiritual demands. It's a rather depressing letter. I have always felt that the States stood as a bulwark between us and military disaster. What will be our fate if the U.S. is ever overcome by another power—perhaps a godless one?"

"I wouldn't worry about that. According to John there's a prophecy given to his church that the country will never become subject to another," Frank said.

"But the promise is given on condition," Esta corrected him. "It will be safe from conquest only as long as its people serve God, and from my observations while I lived there I'd say not many are serving the Almighty."

"Well, I don't believe there's any cause for alarm. History has been repeating itself for ages, and I believe it will continue to do so. All nations have their ups and downs—their periods of prosperity and depression, their times of war and peace—but they usually snap back. The trouble with you, Esta, is that you accept everything Joseph Smith said as fact."

"I wish you could forget the man for a moment and concentrate on what he, through divine inspiration, produced. The Book of Mormon was not written in 1830, you know. It was begun two thousand years before Christ was born."

"That's what your prophet told you!"

"Well, if Joseph Smith wrote the book without the help of God, he was one of the smartest men who has ever lived. Have you finished reading it?"

"I'm almost through, Esta."

"Then you know how many prophecies found there have already been fulfilled. I think the first thing that caught my attention in the book was the revelation concerning the return of the Jews to their homeland. This was to occur after its coming forth. In 1830 when this translation was made there was no sign of this event, yet today thousands of Israelites have returned and redeemed land that for centuries has been considered desert. That fact started my study of the church. I wish we could see Señor Acosta more often. There are so many things I want to discuss with him, and there never seems time enough when I'm in Mexico City. I'd like to know more about the plates that are to be revealed in the future."

"I remember hearing John refer to them. I surmise we'll have to wait a long time before we see that prediction fulfilled, won't we?" Frank asked skeptically.

"Who knows? It may be later than we think."

Chapter 31

Frank sent Esta home early. She had set his meal on the back of the stove to keep warm and reminded him of it when she left, but he was in no mood for eating.

He could hear the children outside as they sat down to their evening meal. The long arbor made a perfect shelter for their summer table. He looked through his opened window. They were seated with bowed heads as Father Martiné asked a blessing on the food. As soon as the "amen" was spoken, all fell to, each arguing over the merits of his contribution to the menu.

Frank's thoughts turned to his own problem. He had come to the end of the book. Only the concluding chapter remained, and he hesitated cutting this last prop from under his arguments. He was afraid that reading would destroy his final objections. At last he grudgingly sat down with it and read:

Now, I Moroni, write somewhat as seems to me good; and I write to my brethren, the Lamanites, and I would that they should know that more than 420 years have passed away since the sign was given of the coming of Christ. And I seal up these records after I have spoken a few words of exhortation to you.

Behold, I would exhort you, when you read these things, if it be wisdom in God that you read them, that you remember how merciful the Lord has been to the children of men.

And if you ask with a sincere heart, with real intent, having faith in Christ, he will manifest the truth unto you.

For the time speedily comes when you shall know that I lie not, for you shall see me at the bar of God, and the Lord will say to you, "Did I not declare my words unto you which were written by this man, like as one speaking out of the dust?"

Frank closed the book and walked out onto his porch and looked toward the mountain. A gentle breeze set the flowers in his garden dancing. He watched their movement for a moment, then lifted his gaze once more to the mountaintop.

"There has to be an answer," he mused, "but I can't find it. Any force that can set that magnificent mountain in place and create such fragile beauty in a flower is capable of accomplishing anything. These are truly miracles, yet I can't accept the miracle of the book. I *must* see John!" He crossed over to the neighboring yard where Esta was sweeping the patio.

"Where's Margarita?" he asked.

"Helping at the hotel. Do you need to see her?"

"Not especially. I have to go into the City right away. Will you see that Antonio looks after my place while I'm away?"

"Of course. Are you ill, Professor? You look pale. . . . Maybe you'd better come in and take a dose of this tonic I made."

"Is that what I smelled cooking over here this afternoon? No, thank you!"

"How long will you be gone?"

"I'll be home Sunday. I want to see John Acosta."

Frank found John at his desk, a sheaf of papers before him. "I've been expecting you," John said. "Sit down."

Frank took the chair offered him. He had felt such an urgency to get to his friend, and now that he confronted him he didn't know what to say.

John broke the silence. "It's been a struggle, hasn't it, Frank?"

"Yes, and it still is. I don't know why. . ."

"It isn't unusual. I suppose the manner in which the book was brought forth is a stumbling block to many people. The idea of an angel revealing its existence is just too much for some to accept."

"Why should it be? We're surrounded by miracles. . . we live on one. What greater wonder can there be than the planets orbiting in their courses? Why should we balk at the visits of angels? I never heard any professing Christian question the story of the angels driving Adam and Eve from the garden, or the heavenly messenger who spoke to Zacharias or to the Virgin Mary. If God is the father of all men, why isn't he as concerned with us and as eager for us to know his will as he was for Moses or Paul?"

A smile formed on John's lips. "You don't have to convert me, Frank," he said.

"I know, but I can't convert myself. I've used all these arguments, and yet. . .John, I'm confused."

"Then you aren't ready for church membership."

"No, but I wish I was. I feel like crying with the father who asked for healing for his son, 'Lord, I believe, help thou my unbelief.' The truth is, John, I want to believe."

John's face brightened. "Then the battle's won, Frank. Isobel will be very happy. Shall I call her? She's on the patio."

But Frank was already halfway across the room. At the door he paused. By moonlight Isobel was training tendrils of a vine through the latticework of the trellis. At the sound of his step she turned.

"Isobel, is it too late to start over? Can't we begin again?" For a moment she stood looking at him, then hurried to his open arms. From the shelter of his embrace she moved her head in firm assent.

———

"Mamá, what are you doing out there in the hot sun? The boys will take care of that."

"I know, Esta, but I *have* to do something. I'm too restless to be idle." Margarita attacked the weeds as though they were a mortal enemy.

"Well, come in and find a job in the house. You'll make yourself sick working like that in this heat. I don't think you're feeling well." Esta took the hoe out of her hands and leaned it against the fence. "I'll have Daniel put it away," she said as she took Margarita's arm and urged her toward the house. "Sit here on the patio while I get you a glass of lemonade. That will cool you off." When she returned Calla was with her. She ran to Margarita and tugged at her skirt.

"I want to sit on your lap, Mamá," she said. "I want some lemonade, too."

"You're a delight, Calla. Why didn't your mother have triplets when she had you? We would have had three times as much pleasure," Margarita told her, hugging her close. Calla responded by drawing Margarita's glass to her lips.

"Don't let her do that. Calla, you leave Mamá's lemonade alone. I'll get you a glass." When Esta returned Calla was in the yard chasing the chickens.

"She didn't really want this, did she?" Esta sat down and began sipping Calla's drink.

"Esta," Margarita said thoughtfully, "I've been very blind, very foolish, very stubborn. Now I think I've made up my mind."

"About what?"

"I'm going into the City to see Grant."

"Good! The bus leaves the hotel in about an hour. I'll pack your bag while you shower and dress."

"There's no need to be in such a rush, Esta. I can go tomorrow."

"No, Mamá, go on that next bus! I don't want you changing your mind again. Hurry now. . .while I lay out your clothes."

Chapter 32

"You have a very sick cow here, Grant."

"I know; that's why I called you. She's valuable, too; I can't afford to lose her."

"Let's get her into the barn so I can treat her."

"All right, Sixto, you and Alex help us get her on her feet."

They were struggling with her when Felicia called Grant to the telephone.

"I can't come now...take the number."

The maid went back to the house and returned almost immediately.

"She says she will wait, Señor, and she's crying."

"A woman...crying? Who can that be?...Gently, boys, gently," Grant cautioned as the men showed a tendency to prod the sick animal into a faster pace.

"It sounds like Señora Marquez," Felicia ventured.

"Margarita!" Grant whirled to face the maid. "It can't be!"

She shrugged her shoulders and retreated.

"Manuel, do whatever is necessary here and send me your bill," Grant said and hurried to the house, where he jerked the door open and let it slam after him. He picked up the phone and shouted his greeting.

It *was* Margarita and she *was* crying.

"Margarita, are you all right?"

"Yes, I'm all right, but I must see you. Can you come to me here?"

"Can I! Are you sure you're all right?"

"Yes, but I must see you, please?"

"Where are you?"

"The Villa Hermosa."

"I'm on my way." A very short time later he was at the hotel desk.

"Hello, Grant. Room 240...you're to go right up."

"Without being announced?"

"That's what Señora Marquez said."

At her invitation Grant entered the room, closing the door behind him. "You wanted to see me, Margarita?"

"Yes. Thank you for coming." For a moment she was silent, then, "I want to apologize for the things I said the last time we were together."

"Forget it, Margarita. You were not well."

"I was perfectly well, Grant. I was just being vindictive. I felt that Pasquelo was growing away from me—that I was losing him completely—and I blamed you for it. I don't know how I could have sent you away when I really do love you." She turned to face him. "Grant, will you marry me?"

"Will I marry you! Will I...." He crossed the room in three long strides and took her in his arms.

For the next half hour they renewed their dreams and hopes and plans. "And this time there'll be no delay. I won't let you leave the City until after we're married," Grant declared.

"I wish you had taken that stand months ago," she replied.

"Hey, Marquez, telephone!"

"Thanks, Marvin. It must be Herman. He was going to call me and give me the score on the ball game. Will you hand me my crutches, Roy? Of all times to sprain an ankle! Just when I'm ready to leave for home," Pasquelo complained as he struggled to his feet.

"Need some help negotiating the stairs?"

"Thanks, I think I can manage. Did Herman say how the game came out?"

"Herman? You mean the phone call? It isn't Herman; it's long distance from Mexico."

"Mexico! My dad! Here, Marv, carry my crutches. I'm going to ride the banisters down."

Marvin complied and ran to the foot of the stairs to raise a barrier in event the newel post failed to stop Pasquelo. The descent was successful and Pasquelo picked up the phone anxiously. Grant was not given to calling.

"Dad, is everything all right at home?"

"I'll say it is! How are you?"

"Oh, fine, except for a sprained ankle."

"Has a doctor seen it?"

"Oh, sure. He taped it and put me on crutches for a week. Then I'll be home."

"Hold on. . . . Your mother heard the word 'doctor,' and if I hadn't had my arm around her she would have fallen in a faint."

"Do you mean that you and Mother . . ."

But Margarita had taken over. "Pasquelo, why did you have to see a doctor?"

"Just a sprained ankle, Mamá. Now what about you and Dad?"

"Are you sure there is nothing more serious? You're not keeping anything from us, are you?"

"No, Mamá, I'm not! Now don't interrupt me again. Are you and Dad . . . ?"

"We've resolved all our difficulties, Pasquelo."

For a moment he was silent. A thousand words clamored to be said, and all he could think of was, "That's nice. . . . I think that's nice."

"And Pasquelo, we were married this morning."

There was no hesitancy now in his expression of approval. "Wow, that's *really* nice!" he shouted, and the happy vibrations carried all the way from Aunt Dump's dining room to the lobby of the Villa Hermosa.